FICTION HOUSE PRESS
PRESENTS

SNAPPY

August 1931
Vol. 10, No. 2

This reprint edition is a facsimile of the original pulp magazine. Variations in printing and quality can be attributed to the original magazine which was printed on rough woodpulp paper. No attempt has been made to politically correct any language deemed inappropriate to the modern reader.

ISBN 978-1-64720-243-9

www.FictionHousePress.com
fictionhousepress@gmail.com

Snappy

Illustrated Fun and Fiction.

VIRGINIA O'DAY
Editor

Vol. 10, No. 2

Published Monthly by
LOWELL PUBLICATIONS, INC.
2757 Euclid Hts. Blvd., Cleveland Hts., Ohio.

25c the Copy

August, 1931

Agents! This Marvelous Invention Will Make Up to $40.00 a Day Easy

Just plug in at the nearest electric outlet and presto!—you have instantaneous, continuous running hot water from your cold water faucet. This tells you in a nutshell why the invention of the Tom Thumb automatic electric hot water heater will make it easy for you to make up to $40.00 a day.

The electric heated steaming hot water comes direct from the faucet instantaneously—yes, as quickly as you can turn on the current and the hot water runs indefinitely until you shut off the electricity. The cost is small—convenience is great. Useful wherever hot water is needed—no fuss or bother—attached to any faucet in a jiffy. Works on either AC or DC current. You and your customers will marvel and be delighted at this new discovery of electrical science. The small cost of $3.75 for the Tom Thumb, Junior (110 volts) or $5.75 for Tom Thumb, Senior (220 volts) does the work of any expensive hot water heating equipment costing several hundred dollars—the Tom Thumb absolutely eliminates the plumber or any other additional expense. Order direct from us! We are the originators, manufacturers, owners and patentees of the famous and original Tom Thumb electric hot water heater.

KITCHEN

SHAVING

BATH

DOCTOR

FACTORY

No Installation—Stick One On Faucet and Sale Is Made

Think of it! No installation, no extra expense—nothing else to do but to stick it on the faucet, turn on electricity and it is there ready for duty. Easily removed when not wanted and easily carried to any part of house where cold water is running and hot water is wanted. Has many uses—too numerous to mention here. Weighs only 1 lb., made entirely of aluminum. Cannot rust, no moving parts, nothing to get out of order.

If $40 A Day Sounds Good To You Rush Coupon

This new scientific invention offers tremendous sales possibilities. At the low price of $3.75 you should be able to sell at least 40 a day. You pocket $1.00 cash commission on every sale. If you would like to know all about this proposition, sign your name and address to coupon or, better still, get started selling at once. Attach money order for $2.75 to coupon and rush to us. We will send complete selling outfit containing 1 Tom Thumb electric hot water heater, order blanks, selling particulars and everything necessary to help you get started making up to $40.00 a day at once.

Terminal Products Co., Inc.

Dept. 2808

200 HUDSON ST.

NEW YORK

Terminal Products Co., Inc.
Dept. 2808, 200 Hudson St.,
New York, N. Y.

The Tom Thumb electric hot water heater looks like a big money maker to me. I am sure interested in knowing how to make up to $40.00 a day with this proposition. I have checked below the proposition I am interested in at this moment.

☐ Enclosed find money order for $2.75. Please send me one Tom Thumb Junior, order blanks and selling information. It is understood upon receipt of this sample outfit I will be permitted to take orders and collect $1.00 cash deposit for every Tom Thumb, Jr. I sell, or $1.50 for every Tom Thumb, Sr. I sell. It is understood I will send the orders to you and you will ship direct to my customers C. O. D. for the balance.

☐ I would like to have additional information before acting as one of your agents. Please send this by return mail free of obligation.

Name..

Street..

City.............................. State...............

Canadians please send cash with order at same price.
Other foreign countries $1.00 extra for each unit cash with order.

An Unpardonable Sin

Must every woman pay the price of a moment's happiness in bitter tears? and years of regret? Must millions of homes be ruined—lovers and sweethearts driven apart—marriages totter to the brink of divorce—the sacred joys of sex relations be denied? YES—just as long as men and women remain ignorant of the simple facts of life.

An Unpardonable Sin is total ignorance of the most important subject in the life of every man and woman—SEX.

AWAY WITH FALSE MODESTY!

Let us face the facts of sex fearlessly and frankly, sincerely and scientifically. Let us tear the veil of shame and mystery from sex and build the future of the race on a new knowledge of all the facts of sex as they are laid bare in plain, daring but wholesome words, and frank pictures in this huge new library of Sex Knowledge.

"MODERN EUGENICS"

39 Chapters—Startling Illustrations

This volume abounds in truthful illustrations and pictures of scientific interest that one seldom, if ever, finds outside of the highly technical medical books which laymen fail to understand. Every picture is true to life.

Learn the TRUTH

544 Pages of startling Secrets

The 544 pages of personal secrets revealed in this astounding work were not put together and assembled by the authors with any thought of spreading obscenity—no, on the other hand, the authors' sincerest belief that modern eugenics is a present-day necessity—their heart-felt wish to carry the message before young and old so they may know the truth prompted them to complete this edition and offer it to those who are deserving of knowing the information therein revealed. If you wish to move onward in life without fear, knowing that you are in the right, fortified with knowledge you are entitled to know, send for your copy today.

EVERYTHING A MARRIED WOMAN SHOULD KNOW

Experience is expensive—you do not have to pay the price—you do not have to suffer—you can know in advance what every married woman should know.

- How to hold a husband
- How to have perfect children
- How to preserve youth
- Warding off other women
- Keeping yourself attractive
- Why husbands tire of wives
- Dreadful disease due to ignorance
- Diseases of women
- Babies and birth control
- Twilight sleep—easy childbirth
- Diseases of children
- Family health guide
- Change of life—hygiene
- Why children die young
- Inherited traits and diseases
- What will you tell your growing girl?
- The mystery of twins
- Hundreds of valuable remedies
- Nursing and weaning
- How to care for invalids

Over 350,000 SOLD

This huge volume of sale enabled us to cut the cost of printing so that you may secure your copy of Modern Eugenics at $2.98 instead of the original price of $5.00. Would YOU risk your health and happiness for the sake of having $2.98 more in your pocket?—Of course not!

Girls! DON'T MARRY

Before You Know All This

The very freedom enjoyed by the present modern girl demands that no secrets be kept from her—yes, those who intend to marry should know:—

- The dangers of petting
- How to be a vamp
- How to manage honeymoon
- Beauty diets and baths
- How to attract desirable men
- How to manage men
- How to know if he loves you
- How to acquire bodily grace and beauty
- How to beautify face, hands, hair, teeth and feet
- How to acquire charm
- How to dress attractively
- Intimate personal hygiene
- How to pick a husband

Important

This work will not be sold to minors. When ordering your book, state your age.

What will you tell the ..... growing child

Will you let your children grow up in the same dangerous ignorance in which you yourself perhaps were reared—or will you guide them safely through puberty by the aid of this truly healthful book?

Secrets for Men

Your opportunities are limited by your knowledge. Your very future—your fate and destiny are guided through the power of your own actions—Modern Eugenics arms you with sex knowledge so as to be your guiding star for your future health and happiness so you will know:—

- Mistakes of early marriages
- Secrets of fascination
- Joys of perfect mating
- How to make women love you
- Bringing up healthy children
- Fevers and contagious diseases
- Accidents and emergencies
- Hygiene in the home
- Limitation of offspring
- Warning to young men
- Dangerous Diseases
- Secrets of sex attraction
- Hygienic precaution
- Anatomy and physiology
- The reproductive organs
- What every woman wants
- Education of the family
- Sex health and prevention

Rush Coupon for this precious book

Another opportunity to secure this marvelous book at almost half regular price may never be offered to you again. Do not be guilty of an Unpardonable Sin. Order your copy today. Sign your name and address to the coupon and forward it to us. It will bring your copy in plain wrapper by return mail—SIGN NOW—do not forget.

PREFERRED PUBLICATIONS, 3106
56 West 45th Street,
New York City.

Please send me "Modern Eugenics" SEALED, in plain wrapper. I will pay $2.98 and postage to the postman on delivery, in accordance with your special half price offer. My age is ....

Name ....

Address..

Orders from Foreign Countries must be accompanied by express or money order of $3.45.

Sorry to detain you . . . but I REALLY must tell you something about the August personalities in this number.

There's Robert Leslie Bellem, for instance, author of *Never Say Dice*. He's a young man of Pasadena, Cal., who suddenly disappointed me by writing that he has a wife.

But won't you be THUR-illed to find out that Algernon Free is just what his name implies! Single? You bet. And do I know him . . . .

Robert Bliss is spending his vacation in Far Rockaway, N. Y., listening to the wild waves—and wild women, too, if I know Bobbie.

One of the gals Bobbie met at the seashore is none other than Nancy Lowe—author of *The Love Hunt*. Maybe *she's* through hunting, now that she's met Bobbie. How these lady authors do come between me and my best friends! Oh, me! Oh, my!

Now go ahead and enjoy the stories in this number—and remember that next month you'll read Jack Woodford, Geoffrey Sayre, Robert Dumont, Sally Delmar, and others you like just as much. Bye Bye!

The Editor

Hiking *to* LOVE

ZOOMING along the road to New York, in his Mercedes, Alan felt a sense of lift and elation that had not been his for many moons. Tied down to a job in Chicago, through his father's insistence that he work for his living, he had been bored to death. Alan's mother had been an actress. Never a very successful one; but what was called a "Good Trooper."

Often she had told him of the one night stands —of the little towns left at dawn, for other little towns; of her never growing tired of seeing new places, new faces. Marriage hadn't agreed with her. She had died at forty-five.

Now Alan, at twenty-eight, was all too definitely sure that he had inherited her thirst for adventure, the wanderlust that had made it nearly impossible for her to settle down to mere marriage.

It was far out on the road, between towns, where there was not a human being in sight, that he spied a moving object ahead of him upon the road. A little lonesome, he pressed his foot down still tighter upon the accelerator; the powerful car shot ahead still faster.

When he came near the moving figure, Alan saw that it was a boy. The boy suddenly turned around and jerked his thumb over his shoulder, as an indication that he was going in the same direction as Alan. Alan stopped the car.

"Hop in," he invited.

The boy obediently climbed into the car. Seated himself at Alan's side. Alan wondered at him. He seemed rather delicate and pale.

"Going far?" Alan asked.

"As far as possible," the other answered.

"'As far as possible!'" Alan echoed. "That sounds as though you were just going, and not thinking of arriving anywhere."

"That's it, precisely," the other admitted.

"Running away from home?"

"Well, not exactly running. My aunt won't care that I'm gone, or bother to trace me. I'm of age."

"You! Twenty-one-!" Alan said, incredulously.

"Why! It's not possible!" The boy suddenly turned to look directly at him. Alan was startled. Such facial beauty in a boy was amazing. Such deep blue, big round eyes. Dainty mouth. Soft skin. Oval shaped face delicately lovely.

"I meant," the other stammered; and there was a soft quality to the voice that suddenly revealed everything to Alan.

"You meant," he put in firmly, "that you are of age, at eighteen." She looked at him, startled.

"There!" she said, "I've gone and given myself away right off. I suppose I was mad to think I could get by with it; but, you see, I figured that it was so hard for a girl to get along; while a boy—so I got some boy's clothes and thought I could—"

"You'd never, never pass for a boy," he told her, very much interested now. "But tell me something about your situation; maybe I can help you."

"There's nothing much to tell," she said in a dull, discouraged tone. My name is Grace. "My mother and father are dead. I lived with an aunt. I've finished high school. Always I've wanted to travel. There was no money. I thought I'd just start out, as a boy could, and see the world.—Thought I'd walk, and hitch hike to New York. Maybe, I thought, I could get a job on one of those cattle boats I read about sometimes, that go over to Europe."

She Was Just a Little Girl Who Wanted to See the World

By
JACK
WOODFORD

"Such lovely things—oh, goody!"

"A perfectly wild idea," he said, sternly; "why! there's no telling what might happen to you. You mustn't think of it at all. You must let me take you right back home."

"Oh, no!" she urged; "nothing like that. I couldn't stand that. When I told my aunt I thought of going, she told me to go ahead, that I'd soon come back, when I got hungry. She'd make life utterly miserable for me now."

"Then you must let me help you," he ended up. "If I step on it, we can reach New York in two or three hours. Really, I'd love to help you. I've wanted to travel and see the world myself—but I'm tied down too. It isn't money, in my case—there's plenty of that. It's just my Dad's absurdly fanatical notion that I must plug away at the business, to learn it from the ground up. I'm on a month's vacation, now; had the very devil of a time talking him out of it."

She was watching him with her big, round, beautiful eyes. Tall and dark, and dashingly good looking at twenty-eight, Alan saw that he wasn't registering poorly in her eyes. "If I could help you I'd get a big kick out of it. Will you let me?"

"And what must I do in return?" she asked quietly. He was silent for a moment.

"Just trust me," he told her.

"All right," she said; "but please be nice to me; I've been so unhappy all my life. And there's never been anything in the nature of an *affair*, with me. Of course, some harmless kissing and necking, in high school—but I've always been good, because I was afraid to be any other way."

"WOULD you mind taking off your cap?" Alan asked. She took it off. Looked with breathless appreciation upon a wealth of silky golden hair, cut like a boy's; the unruly natural curl in it was inevitably girlish.

"And you hoped to pass for a boy with that!" he said, grinning.

"I guess it was foolish," she admitted.

"Listen, little fellow," he said; "you can really trust me. I'm not, by nature, a trustable sort of chap, where pretty women are concerned. But you're just a kid, and completely helpless, I wouldn't think of taking advantage of such a situation. The first thing we've got to do is get you some clothes. We'd better go to a hotel in New York and register you. Probably, in the shuffle, with your cap on, you'll pass as a boy. Those boy togs you've got are pretty convincing at a distance. You can wait in a lobby while I register for both. Then I'll go out and round up some clothes for you."

"But why," she protested, "should you spend all that money on me?"

"Adventure," he told her; "where, for the same money, could one buy an equivalent degree of adventure? I thought my vacation might prove more or less a bore; but with you, it's going to prove splendid."

In New York, Alan drove to a hotel and, uneventfully registered for both of them. There were no difficulties. The elevator was crowded so that the bell hop had his hands full and paid no attention to Alan's companion. In the room she walked to the window and looked out, until the bell hop, well tipped, had left the room.

"Now," said Alan, "I must go shopping for you. Make up a list for me, won't you?"

She sat down and made up a list. Handed it to him, blushingly. He looked it over inquiringly, could make little out of it. On most of the items she had an indication as to size; he would simply have to do his best and trust to luck, Alan decided. She had jotted down one dress; he decided to get several, so that surely one out of the lot would fit her; and the rest, did they not, could be exchanged.

His shopping tour was a revelation to Alan. Not ever could he remember having gotten more of a kick out of anything than in the buying of the dainty things that she would wear. Instead of a single set of under things, he got a half a dozen, pretty, sleazy, dainty colored things, the very sight of which made his senses run riot. When he returned she was awaiting him anxiously.

"Gee! you were gone so *long!*" she objected. "It was lonesome."

"Shhhhh!" he warned, hearing footsteps in the hall, "they're coming with the packages."

Two taxi drivers who had come up the back freight elevators, assisted by several hotel boys, carried in the packages and piled them up against the wall. Tipping them all generously, so that no suspicions might be raised, Alan stood at last alone in the room with the many packages and the girl. With boyish enthusiasm he pulled some of them open.

She gasped and exclaimed anew over each purchase revealed. There was, beside the clothing, a bottle of expensive perfume and other toilette articles. A dainty platinum wrist watch had taken Alan's eye in a jewelry store. Recklessly he had bought it. Her eyes became even larger when she saw it, draped it over her slender wrist. There was also a pretty string of imitation pearls that had cost plenty, even though they were imitations.

"I should have taken a suite," Alan said, reflectively. "Now I'll have to go downstairs and hang around while you dress."

"Oh please!" she begged; "don't do that. I feel so frightened all alone here, as though somebody were going to come in and arrest me or something. Couldn't you just look out of the window?"

"ALL right," Alan said. "I'll promise not to chance being turned into a pillar of salt." She laid a full selection of the pretties out on the bed, and Alan went over to the window.

"Never before have I had anything like this," she told him rapturously, as she undressed. "Such lovely things—I wonder how I'll feel in them." Her voice was that of a happy child attending its first circus.

One by one he could hear her throwing things off. He kept his eyes glued upon the moving things down in the street, although he was mightily tempted to turn. That slim white body

She was obviously pleased and flattered.

behind him would, he knew, be something extraordinary to look upon.

Suddenly there came a sharp knock at the door. She let out a frightened,

"Oh!"

Involuntarily Alan turned. Before him he saw the most beautiful symposium of feminine flesh that ever it had been his good fortune to behold.

"Who is it?" Alan called through the door.

"Ice Water, Sir," came a voice through the door; one of the bell hops had conceived the valid idea of e x t o r t i n g still another half dollar from the generous new guest. Alan went to the door, opened it far enough to permit the handing in of the water pitcher, tipped the boy and closed the door. Since the bed and the place where she was standing was well out of range of the door it would have been impossible for the boy to see anything.

"I'm awfully sorry," Alan told her, without looking toward her, as he walked back toward the window. "It was quite involuntary, I assure you; and I just want to say that you are more beautiful than I had dreamed it was possible for a girl to become."

"Oh! Do you really think so!" she said, obviously pleased and flattered. There was a pause; and then she said,

"You may look now, if you like."

He turned again and beheld her, clad in the

She let out a frightened "Oh!"

flimsy underthings she had selected first to don. They covered her lightly, diaphanously. She had selected the pink things; and against the delicate pink, her well turned shoulders, snow white bosom, and slender flanks appeared snow white and satin soft.

Alan knew that his appreciation was literally glowing in his eyes. He saw her look into his eyes and then become just a little bit frightened.

"Please give me a chance to dress," she suggested.

"I guess you're right," Alan said hastily, and turned to the window.

In another ten minutes she was completely dressed. She had chosen a light green afternoon frock. It fit perfectly. She had also put on the wrist watch and the beads. So pretty she was that Alan was literally unstrung. He trembled as he walked toward her.

"You lovely thing," he said, in a low tone, "what ever shall I do with you? I had in mind giving you some money, and sending you on your way toward adventure; but you're too delicate and tender and lovely to face the world alone. I'm afraid you're going to be considerable worry to me; for I shan't be happy a moment until I know how you're going to be taken care of and protected."

"Oh! Really!" she objected, "I won't let myself be a worry to you. You've been so nice. It would be awful if, in return, I became just a nuisance to you. I'll go away—I'll disappear and you can forget all about me."

"I can *never* forget all about you," Alan told her with conviction. "It's not at all possible."

Fortunately, in the hotel Alan had chosen, there were no floor clerks. When, later, he took her down to dinner, nobody seemed to see anything unusual about the matter except that the young girl with Alan was an extraordinarily beautiful and winsome one.

After dinner they took in a show. Grace, never having seen a legitimate stage production before, was wildly enthusiastic. Almost unconsciously she slipped cool fingers into Alan's hand. He sat holding them ecstatically. He could never remember having felt quite that way toward a girl before; sort of choky and sadly happy.

After the theatre they went to a night club; and, very late, at nearly two in the morning, left the night club in a taxi cab.

"Now," Alan told her, "comes the difficult part. Probably there'll be nothing said at the hotel; there will be a different set of clerks, of course, on duty—but, you see, I'll have to slip out and go to some other hotel, because if I were to ask for a separate room now they'd surely think there was something uncommonly queer going on."

She clung to his hand in sudden fright.

"Will I have to stay there alone!" she wailed. "Oh gee! Now I'm in the devil of a fix. I'll be terrified there alone; and yet I'd be afraid too if you were to stay. I'd never make a real adventuress—I see it perfectly plainly now. I had just imagined things. Oh! What'll I do! I can't go back to my aunts. I can't stay in New York. There's simply not any place in the world for me."

He put his arm around her.

"Listen," he said, emphatically, "you're not to worry. I'll get you out of this somehow. You're not to be frightened tonight. Tomorrow we'll think things over. Perhaps I'll find you a cozy little apartment in New York somewhere, and get you a maid, until you get [*Continued on page* 62]

Jailer (to prisoner awaiting execution): "You have an hour of grace."
Prisoner: "O. K. Bring her in."

◆◆

He: "I think you are beautiful."
She: "But my clothes are against me."
He: "Sure—that's why I think you're so beautiful."

"Did your girl friend make the train?"
"No—only the conductor."

She: "Are you looking at my knee?"
He: "Aw, g'wan. You know I'm above that!"

He: "Do you know the secret of popularity?"

She: "Yes, but mother says that I mustn't."

◆◆

He asked his girl friend to his apartment.
"I can't say no," she responded.
"Better not come, then," he advised.

◆◆

They called her arrow, because she quivered before every beau.

ARTIN ACKROYD motored up to the house in the woods, hunted through a bunch of keys he had been given; found one that fitted the garage door, and put his car away.

He stopped for a minute, after having done this, and stood looking around him. Before him was the house, solid and comfortable looking; and all around him was virgin woods. Not a sound, save the notes of a few birds. In the car were provisions to last for at least a week. He would come out to the garage and lug them in later.

There were, Hayden had told him, no servants in the house; for this Ackroyd was supremely

grateful; he wanted, more than anything else in the world, to get away from everybody.

Hunting through the bunch of keys again, he found one that fitted the front door. He entered, went upstairs and selected a bedroom. Hayden had informed him that the one servant left in charge of the house, an old woman who cooked when Ackroyd was there alone, and who cleaned up, had left suddenly on account of the death of a sister. She wouldn't be back for a week.

He still remembered how to cook the simple things that he would need; for, at military school, when he was a boy, cooking had been one of the fine arts, taught in military schools.

In the basement, Hayden had told him, was a swimming pool. Before doing anything else, Ackroyd decided, he would go down for a swim. He felt, he told himself, a thousand years old after three of the most hectic months he had ever spent in his life on the New York Stock Exchange; three months of falling market! But a glance into the nearest mirror belied his thoughts about himself.

He was thirty-five, and looked thirty; his shiny black hair, meticulously parted on the side, without a single strand misplaced, had no tinge of gray. There were no creases of care anywhere upon his handsome face. His eyes were bright and youthful, and his figure erect and military. A little reassured, he decided that a week of rest would do wonders for him. Undressing swiftly, he grabbed up a bathrobe and descended the stairs.

THE pool, he decided, might not be filled; but Hayden had assured him it was easy to fill it by simply turning on the taps.

In the basement he walked along a corridor until he found an open door. He looked through. To his surprise the room was lighted. "Darn careless of Hayden," he said to himself, "to have left the lights on; or maybe that old woman who cooks —" He entered the room.

The pool, he saw, was also full of water. And then he stood rooted to the spot with amazement.

There was something floating in the center of the pool. Ackroyd's eyes dilated; his breath came in short gasps. A dead body! Somebody had committed—! But no, it was no dead body. What a lovely little head; slim, pink white torso, tapering thighs; what utter and complete perfection!

She was floating with most of her body under water, perfectly motionless; eyes closed, ears covered with water, so that she could hear nothing. Ackroyd took another close look, and then blushed crimson. He was getting quite a kick, or had been, he decided, over the lovely, nude body of a mere child, a girl, perhaps, of fourteen or sixteen.

His attitude toward the object of such high visibility changed; his pleasure of contemplation now, he told himself, was merely one of the aesthetic realm of thought.

Appreciative of the beautiful, he admired the way her slim young body fitted together, a perfect rhythm in flesh; young girls, he sighed, were so often like that; and when they grew older, they got out of proportion someway.—Some neighborhood urchin, he supposed; who, knowing that the house was temporarily deserted, that Hayden had divorced his wife and gone in to the city to live, had taken advantage of the pool, breaking in somewhere, through some basement window probably. He looked around for her clothes; they were nowhere to be found.

Darned dangerous, he decided, for a child to be playing all alone in a tank like that—suppose she got cramps, or something. He decided to tell her what he thought of such foolishness and send her home. He called out loudly. Her ears under the water, she did not hear him.

He walked around to the other side of the tank. Kneeled down on the marble edge, reached far out, touched her. The result of this was devastating. She thrashed around in the water horribly. Ackroyd watched her for a moment in perplexity, before the full significance of what had happened came over him. The touch had so startled and frightened her that she had gulped a lung full of water. She was strangling.

When this realization hit him, he forgot all other considerations; threw aside his bathrobe and dived in, since her thrashings in the water had carried her out of reach from the edge of the pool. In the water, he clasped the tiny body firmly from behind, and worked toward the iron stairway out of the pool with great difficulty, for she was struggling frantically, endeavoring to seize him around the neck; if she succeeded in this, they would both drown, he knew.

He stopped working toward the ladder, and treaded water; meanwhile holding her from behind, tightly against him. She kept on struggling for several moments, then suddenly stopped and went limp. Ackroyd then, with a few swift strokes, reached the ladder with her and climbed out.

It seemed to him that she was weightless as he sped upstairs with her in his arms. In the large front living room he stopped. She was still "out." —What to do now!

He ransacked his mind for the life saving instructions he had received at military school. They came back vaguely. He put her down upon the rug, face downward; grasped her firmly midriff; leaned over, raised her torso gently, lowered her; raised her, lowered her; presently she let out a strangley cough, and a quantity of water came out upon the rug. At this, she rolled over and groaned feebly.

WITH her lying on her back now, Ackroyd leaned over her, grasped both of her arms; pulled them down until her elbows pressed beneath her lungs, then raised them far above her head, flat upon the floor. He repeated this motion several times. She groaned again. Her eyes opened; she gasped; began breathing steadily.

And then he saw that she had fully regained consciousness and had given him an amazed and shocked stare. Realizing the reason for the amaze-

She grabbed the big glass and tossed it off with one swallow.

ment and shock in her eyes, he left her and sprinted back down into the basement for his bathrobe. Securing it, and draping it around him properly, he hurried back upstairs.

She was sitting up on the floor now, looking dazed, and breathing with difficulty. She looked up at him as he entered.

"Well, child, you certainly got yourself into a fine mess," Ackroyd said, reprovingly. "You ought to be ashamed of yourself, a little girl like you, breaking into other people's houses and using their swimming pools. You might have drowned with nobody around to do anything about it. I'm very much ashamed of you. If you were my little girl, I'd give you a good spanking. Where are your clothes?"

"Upstairs," she said weakly, "in the first guest room in the hall at the top of the stairs."

"I'll get them," Ackroyd told her; "lie down and rest while I'm gone, and try to get up strength enough to dress. I'll help you."

He went upstairs. On a chair by a bed there was a heap of wispy clothing. Without being able to make head or tail of it, he grabbed up the whole bunch and went downstairs. She had followed his instructions, was lying on her side.

Darned beautiful things, children, Ackroyd said to himself; if there were anywhere in the world a grown woman as pretty as that—! He went and stood over her.

"Can you stand up?" he asked. She nodded weakly and got dizzily to her feet. Ackroyd hunted through the clothing. The pink wispy stuff, he supposed, went first. He held it up and tried to

"I'm nineteen," she said.

figure out how to get it on her. While he was trying to decide she grabbed it and wriggled into it. Ackroyd was startled.

Funny what a mature appearance it gave her; and, astonishingly, the addition of the pink, wispy underthing, faintly tinged with perfume, actually added to her loveliness, rather than subtracting from it through concealment.

She sat down on the floor and reached for her stockings. Pulled them on. Sheer black stockings against milk white skin; and dainty little band garters just above fully rounded dimpled knees.

Knowing little of the magics of femininity, having had no sisters and no sweethearts, so far, Ackroyd was astonished that the stockings somehow added to her seeming maturity, and actually added to her loveliness; he wouldn't have believed that the putting on of things could have made feminine loveliness more poignant even than complete—!

She was evidently feeling better now. She got into her frock. Leaned far over, squeezed the water out of her hair.

"My shoes—" she asked, weakly. He looked around; saw that he had forgotten them. Went back upstairs. Found a towel for her hair, and the shoes.

It was when she put on the high heeled shoes, and became instantly much taller, and perfectly poised as to figure, that Ackroyd thoroughly realized for the first time that she was no child.

"Say!" he got out, "how old are you?"

"Nineteen," she gasped, still not quite recovered from her shock. "There's some whiskey out in the cupboard in the kitchen, in a little keg; lying on its side, with a wooden faucet stuck into it. Go draw me some, will you please?"

"I certainly will," Ackroyd told her; "I need some myself." He found the liquor in the cupboard; drew one large, generous drink for himself, and a tiny one for her.—Returned to the living room. Before he could hand her either, she grabbed the big glass from him and tossed it off with one swallow.

"Oh boy!" she got out, her childish voice roughened with the whiskey, "now I begin to feel like somebody. Say! What the devil do you mean by poking your finger into me when I'm floating, supposedly alone in the house, and scaring me half to death, huh?—And who the heck are you, and how did you get in here anyway, and what do you mean by wrestling with me when I was dying; and trying to yank off my arms—and is that all the whiskey you're going to drink?

"Not that you're so bad looking even if you are a burglar. My name's Magda—what's yours and when did you come and how did you get in."

"Yes indeed," Ackroyd told her, helplessly.

"Well, that explains everything," she said; "but I could stand another drink, I've had a great shock." Ackroyd handed her the other glass.

"A *drink!* I said. What are you handing me that unwashed glass with something in the bottom of it for." Helplessly Ackroyd went back to the cupboard and drew two large drinks of liquor from the keg. Returned to the living room.

She was drying her hair. He handed her the drink. She tossed it off carelessly, as before; he tossed off his—felt heaps better fitted to face the unusual situation.

"Sit down and I'll help you with your hair," he told her. She sat down and he got behind her and rubbed with the towel. Went upstairs, got another towel; rubbed some more. Her hair began to dry and become spun gold in his hand. Rubbing her head seemed to have some sort of hypnotic effect upon her. [*Continued on page* 60]

ON THE BEACH

Oh, how they loiter,
How they saunter,
How they linger
On the beach

The pretty misses,
Smiling maidens,
Flirting damsels
On the beach

How they captivate,
Charm and fascinate,
How they seek a mate
On the beach

—EDNA GAY

UPPOSE, snappy reader, that the girl you loved madly and who had always said "No!" insisted on coming up to your apartment one night at midnight even though you told her over the phone that you were in bed. What would you think? What would you expect?

As Carter Lyons put down the bedside phone, got out and slipped into a dressing-gown, his head was literally spinning with joy.

"All things come to him who waits!" he murmured prowling about the living-room, putting the pillows on the divan to rights, trying a dozen different effects with the lights to obtain the most love-provoking effect.

He had indeed waited a long time for Margie Wilson. He had met her at a strip-poker game and the sight of her rosy complexion—Margie was a rotten poker-player—had made his blood race. That very night, or early morning rather, he had taken her home. She had let him kiss her a couple of dozen times—and that was all.

For weeks he had laid siege. And he had never gotten beyond the stage of acquaintanceship he had achieved the first night.

For Margie's price for any real intimacy was far beyond what he wanted to pay. She wanted marriage.

It had made Carter's blood run cold the way she expatiated on the joys of wedded life. Marriage! All he had observed of that institution had confirmed him in the belief that bachelorhood was nature's greatest gift to man. No girl of the innumerable pretties who had perfumed his life with their kisses and love-joy had succeeded in trapping him into marriage. And even though he wanted Margie as he had never wanted any girl before, he would not pay that price.

So he said "No!" and Margie said "No!" and in a huff he went off to Europe for three months, and when he got back the first bit of news he heard was that Margie had married Tom Wilson, the big stock-broker.

Carter had taken it greatly to heart. For some reason he felt that he had been let out. The least Margie could have done would have been to notify him of her intentions to marry Tom and give Carter a chance to change his mind.

"I'm not through yet," swore our hero. "Someday Margie will belong to me. She hasn't played fair, leading me on—and then marrying another guy!"

But Margie as a wife was twice as circumspect as Margie, the single girl. She wouldn't even permit Carter to kiss her for old times' sake. Carter stopped coming to see her. He busied himself with more approachable young ladies and tried to

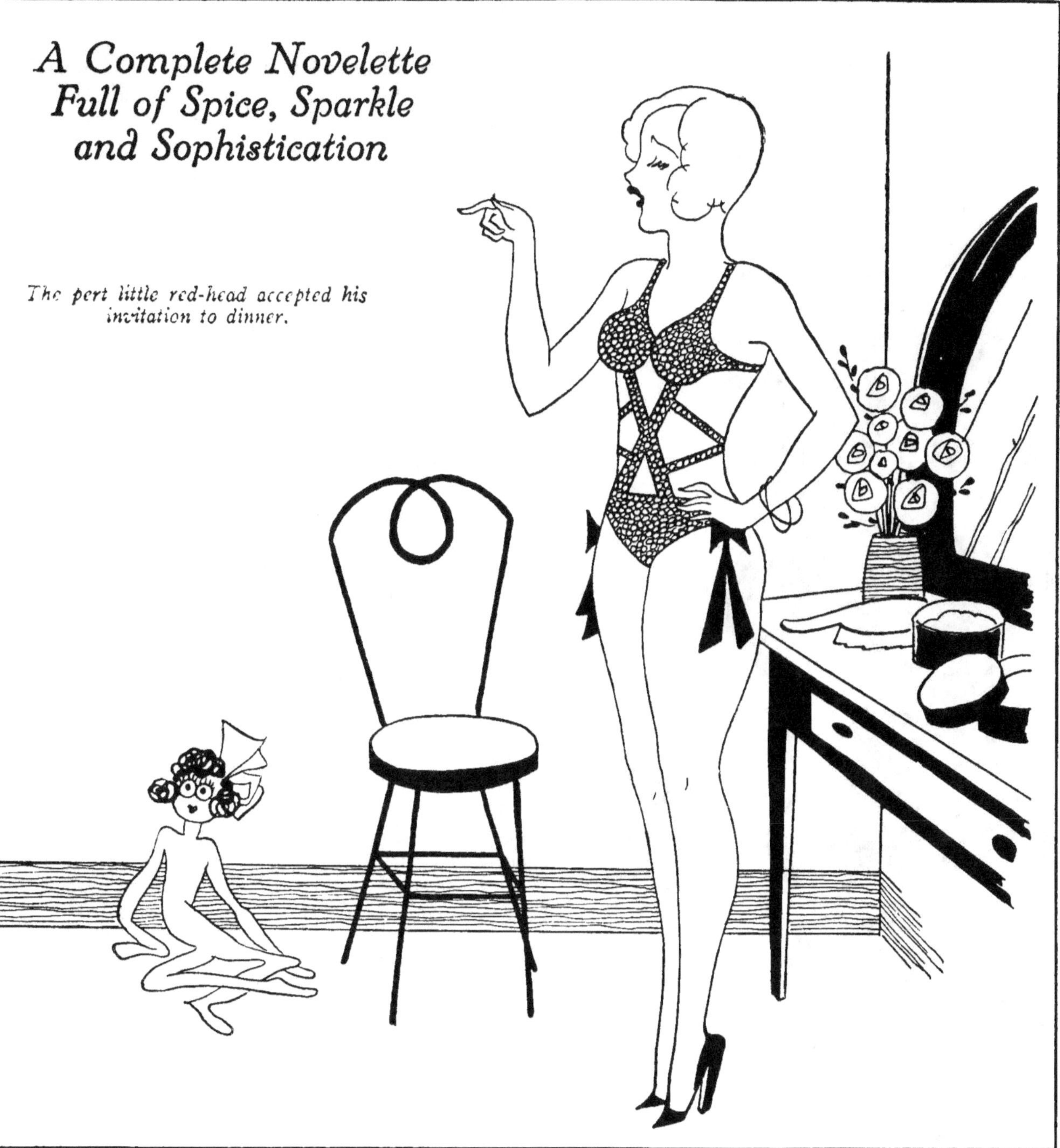

The pert little red-head accepted his invitation to dinner.

forget her. And then, when he had almost succeeded, came the merry jingle of the phone that preluded Margie's voice insisting that she was going up to see him at once.

And here was the knock at the door that announced Margie herself.

As she came into the room, Carter's eyes devoured her hotly. His lips burned to do likewise. She was beautiful. Her eyes were deep pools of black in her exotically pallid face. Marriage had even improved her figure, giving just the added few curves to her slimness that made it perfect.

"Hello, Carter!" she faltered.

Carter felt it his duty to disabuse her of the idea that she wasn't welcome. Advancing swiftly, he took her in his arms. For a moment she went limp in his arms and he even fancied that her soft lips were responding to the steel-hard pressure of his own. Then she struggled out of his clasp.

"No, Carter—you mustn't—really!"

"I'm sorry," said Carter quietly. "Sit down, Margie. Let me get you a drink."

"No, thanks." She dropped upon the divan. She took a silk inch of handkerchief out of her bag

"What do you mean by two-timing me?"

and dabbed at her eyes. "Carter, I'm in trouble. You've got to help me," she said. She turned her moistly luminous eyes upon him. "You're the only one I can possibly come to, Carter."

"I'm glad you came, no matter what the reason."

She smiled faintly at that. "It's Tom," she said. "We—we're having trouble."

"What else did you expect when you married him," said Carter tartly. "You didn't expect a man like Tom Wilson to appreciate you, did you? It may sound caddish, but if you had thought twice before throwing yourself into his arms—"

"It isn't that Tom doesn't love me," said Margie. "The trouble is that his nature is too ardent altogether. He's infatuated with a girl in the Nudities. Oh, Carter, I hope it isn't too much to ask, but I want you to—to help me cure him of that infatuation. I love him. I'll die if he runs off with her."

And Margie dissolved into tears.

Carter stared at her in amazement. "You want me of all people to help restore your husband to your loving arms. Why, Margie, don't you realize how much I care for you?"

"I do. That's why I came to you. You're the only friend I have in the world," she sobbed.

Carter took several heated turns about the room.

"Very well," he found himself saying, "just what do you want me to do?"

Margie let her eyes rest upon his for a second, wistful, passionate, haunted. Then:

"I want you to win her away from him," she said with determination.

Carter sat down abruptly. "What!" he babbled. "You want me to win your husband's sweetheart away from him—so that you and he may become reconciled. Margie, do you think I'm made of wood?"

She sighed, gathered up her bag, and started for the door. The way her hips swayed, the irresistible movements of soft flesh outlined by the sheer silk of her gown, set Carter's blood pounding. Besides, his agile brain had pounced upon an idea even while it was whirling with amazement at her proposal to make everything all right in the Wilson household.

"But for your sake I'll do it, Margie. I'll do anything in the world for you." he called out.

She turned. She gave him both her soft little hands.

"I'll never forget it, Carter. Never as long as I live."

And that was how Carter Lyons, young man-about-love, began, for the sake of a woman he couldn't have, a mad pursuit of a girl he didn't want.

Her name was Midgie. She did several solo bits in the big bust-and-hip show known as the Nudities. In these she was clad much like Kipling's boy friend Gunga Din, that is to say she wore "not very much before, and little less than half of that behind." Carter distinctly did not fancy her and he wondered how Tom could prefer her to Margie. He winced at the idea of trying to get to close quarters with the little dancer. Still for Margie's sake it had to be done.

And for his own sake as well.

After he had sent his card in behind scenes with

a scribbled invitation for supper, he treated himself to several appreciative little inner laughs at the cleverness of the idea he had of how to turn Margie's need to his own advantage.

His invitation to supper was accepted. But as he entered Midgie's dressing-room, the pert little red-head said at once:

"I'll go bite an oyster with you, big boy, but no strings attached. You're oak, of course, but I've got a sugar-boy who's out of town. If you want to help make me forget the lonesome blues, I'm yours for an hour, but I go home alone, get me."

"It shall be an honor to console you for your friend's absence with a bite of supper," said Carter in his gravest manner.

They proceeded to a quiet night-club where only six fights and nine drunks enlivened the evening. Midgie, despite her loneliness, ate with good appetite and drank with neat thirst. The liquor seemed to make her melancholy. At the end she had what can only be described as a weeping jag.

"What's troubling you?" asked Carter sympathetically. "Anything I can do?"

"It's my sugar-boy!" wept Midgie. "I love him—oh, I love him. But he won't keep his promises to me. He says he wants to marry me—but every time I talk Municipal Building, he talks about what pretty brassieres I wear or sumpin'. Why does he treat me like that, hey? I want to know."

"Well, I can tell you," said Carter quietly.

"You? Who are you?" asked Midgie belligerently.

"Never mind," said Carter. "But I can tell you why Tom Wilson can't marry you."

Midgie was startled almost into sobriety.

"Who told you about Tom?" she gaped.

"That's not important," said Carter. "Anyhow, he can't marry you at present unless he commits bigamy. But don't let that worry you. I've got a little plan that will help you."

"I'm hearing things!" decided Midgie. She looked almost frightened.

"You will if you listen."

He braced Midgie with another shot of Scotch and spoke earnestly to her for ten full minutes. Midgie's eyes grew wider and wider.

"You want Tom Wilson to marry me!" she exclaimed. "You want him to divorce his wife. Say, where is the needle in the haystack?"

"I'm in love with Mrs. Wilson," said Carter simply. "If he knocks her for a Reno, I'll be her little Nevada knight."

Midgie fell back and laughed.

"Boy, you're all there," she said. "You should be knocking out scenarios for the fillums."

Midgie listened calmly.

"Well how about it?" asked Carter. "Are you with me?"

"Can a fish bark?" asked Midgie. "No. Well, that's how I feel about you, big boy."

Which was her quaint way of swearing allegiance to him, Carter knew, and so forthwith began the comic epic of the great grand passion between Carter Lyons and Midgie La Verne.

Carter's plan was simplicity itself. It was merely what Margie had begged him to do. But with one difference. Margie wanted him to win Midgie away from Tom. As Carter and Midgie planned it, Carter would pursue Midgie, but only in order to arouse Tom to the point where he would insist on running off with Midgie.

And so during the following week, Carter openly gave the world to understand he was infatuated with Midgie. He was present at every performance at which she danced. He took her to all the prominent night-clubs and soon be became known as Midgie's sugar-papa. Which wasn't so, of course. For all Midgie's kissable contours, Carter went to bed every night dreaming of Margie.

BY THE time Tom returned to New York, the affair between Midgie and Carter was so hot on the surface of it, that he hit the ceiling. He lost no time in storming into Midgie's boudoir.

"Who is this guy and what do you mean by two-timing me?" he demanded.

"Do you expect me to wait till the cows amble home till you divorce your ball-and-chain and marry me?" she queried coldly.

"Oh, you know about my wife!"

"A little bird told me."

"Well—a divorce can't be arranged in a day."

Midgie hummed a little tune. Tom gazed at her thoughtfully.

"Right, Midgie," he said. "I haven't played fair with you. But to-night I'm going to think things over carefully. To-morrow I'm coming to see you—to give you a very important decision. Promise me you'll come right home from the theatre and that you'll be alone."

"Of course," cooed Midgie.

But after he had gone, she leaped to the phone, called Carter.

"I want you to be in my apartment to-morrow at eleven-thirty. Oak? You've got to make love to me as you've never made love before to any girl. And listen, big boy—bring a revolver. I've got a grand idea!"

She spoke at length. Carter listened with attention.

"We can't lose," ended Midgie. "Now be on time."

He was. Promptly at eleven-thirty he entered Midgie's boudoir. She was walking up and down restlessly. In her long, slightly bouffant dress of green satin, she was a piquant little figure. But her beauty was lost on Carter.

"Is Tom here?" he queried in businesslike tones.

"No. He phoned that he was delayed. We'll have time to do a little rehearsing for the grand act that will bring my boy friend to his knees."

"What do you mean, rehearse?" asked Carter.

"Well, I don't know how you make love," said Midgie. "And I'm not going to have the show queered because you may not love up to specifications. Suppose you come over here and kiss me the way you will when Tom arrives."

Carter looked at her coral lips without interest.

"I never kiss girls who wear as much clothes as you've got on," he said.

"That's a good point," said Midgie.

Cooly she divested herself of her dress and stood before him in silken chemise, the scantiest of step-ins, and a peach-colored brassiere.

It was really too bad that Carter had only Margie in his mind, or he might have gotten a thrill from the sight of Midgie's lovely white shoulders, the trim shapely legs, the inches of white flesh that showed here and there.

Nor was Midgie thrilled by the act of removing a few clothes in the presence of a man. She had been on the stage too long.

"Is this o. k.?" she asked.

"Now if I kiss you, I guess it will look realistic to your boy friend," he agreed.

"I'll say so," said Midgie. "Well, show me a sample of your kisses."

Carter took her gently into his arms, but without feeling any particular emotion. His lips joined hers. After an interval she drew away.

"That kiss wouldn't fool a child in arms," she said indignantly. "Now try again, and put pep into it."

Carter held her so close that she could hardly breathe. The pressure of his lips this time was enough to satisfy any girl.

"Pretty good," said Midgie. "Now, did you bring the gun?"

"Yes." Carter patted his hip pocket.

"And you've got a good passion-spiel ready?"

"You'll be surprised."

"Fine. Now we've got nothing to do till Tom comes. Do you want to read a good book or something?"

"No. I'll look out of the window—what's that?"

It was the sound of a door opening and closing.

"It's Tom!" cried Midgie. "To my arms, big boy!"

CARTER grasped her and held her softness tight. His lips explored the soft curves of her lips with as much fervor as an expert could simulate.

"I beg pardon." It was a feminine voice, faltering, apologetic. The maid!

"What—only you!" cried Midgie. "Didn't Mr. Wilson just come in?"

"No, Miss. It was only me!" And she ran out of the room at her mistress' murderous glare.

"How dare you?" she screamed.

"A good kiss wasted!" moaned Midgie. "Now we'll have to do it all over again. If I wasn't so much in love with Tom, big boy, I could never go through with this."

"And if I didn't love his wife so much, do you think I could stand it?" retorted Carter.

At this moment the maid put her head in at the door.

"Mr. Wilson!" she announced breathlessly.

Midgie tousled her hair and pulled a shoulder strap down. Carter leaped over to her and locked her in a crushing embrace.

"Tom's at the door!" whispered Midgie to him quickly as she relaxed in his arms. "Now go to it, big boy. Loud and strong."

Carter took the cue at once.

"I love you!" he cried loud enough to be heard through a dozen doors. "I know it was wrong of me to break in on you like this, but I can't help it. I love you! I love you!"

Midgie permitted his lips to crush hers for one moment. Then she fought away.

"How dare you!" she screamed realistically for the benefit of Tom Wilson who was standing as if stupified at the door. "Get away from me. I detest you! Oh—" She pretended to be seeing Tom for the first time. She ran to him. "Tom—Tom, protect me from this maniac. He broke into my boudoir while I was dressing. He says he loves me."

[*Continued on page 56*]

She was only a Spaniard's daughter, but she had a beautiful Pyrenees.

◆◆

She: ***"I wouldn't kiss the best man going."***
He: ***"No—but coming back you'll change your mind."***

◆◆

She: "I hate to be pawed over and kissed."
He: "All right with me. I'll kiss you first."

"How much do you love me?"
"Terribly mush."

Nice Sneeze!

"My boy friend has two faults."
"You and who else?"

◆◆

Two sugar daddies, who had not seen each other for quite some time, chanced to meet.
"How you've changed!" said one. "What makes you look so old?"
"Trying to keep young," was the reply.
"Trying to keep young?"
"Yes—three of them."

◆◆

You can always tell a lady by the way she dresses—but a real lady would pull down the shades.

MALOU Gets Her Man

You'll Like This Zippy Little Story Of A Frisky Little Girl

By ALGERNON FREE

"Now what shall I do?"

IF THERE was anything Malou loved, it was swimming in the "altogether."

When she was a little girl, she had lived out in the country, and there had been a pond on her father's farm. Nobody else ever went near it, and, many times, she had gone to swim in it au natural. The memory of these happy childhood days had always lingered, even though Malou now had grown into a splendid, clean limbed, lithe young lady of twenty.

One reason she had accepted an invitation to the Torrenton's house party was that she knew of the splendid, large cement pool behind the house, beautifully shaded by tall trees, and just a step or two from the house.

Malou had retired at one o'clock; but she hadn't gone to sleep. It was hot in the house. The party had been a hot one. Even the cocktails had made her hotter. She lay awake in bed, tossing and turning, thinking of that cool cement tank not far behind the house.

She listened intently. Everyone seemed to have retired now. There was not a sound anywhere, and the Torrenton's, she knew, kept no dogs.

Rising, she turned on the light. Stepped out of her pajamas. Got, from an upper drawer where she had put it when she unpacked for a week end, her brief, black, knit bathing suit. She was about to slip into it when she caught sight of herself in the full length mirror on the back of the door.

And what a sight it was. A long, slim, clean limbed body, built for speed. A body topped by a small, well shaped head, and a face as pretty as the law of nature in such matters allows. A face equipped with twin, large, blue eyes; fitted with eyelids that contained long, cheek dusting lashes. A tiny, hollow equipped neck; beautifully rounded and dimpled shoulders. A flat, soft white torso.

HER hips were narrow, and her thighs were svelte and sleek. She discarded the bathing suit and decided to take a chance. Everybody was in bed. Tiptoeing carefully from the room she went downstairs, through the long hall that led to the rear, and found the kitchen. There was bright moonlight outside, and its argent light penetrated at the windows so that, with her eyes accustomed to the dark, she could see quite clearly.

Without difficulty she found and opened the back door. Stepped out upon the path that led to the pool. Not a sound had she heard so far. She wished that modern life were just a trifle more daring than it is, so that she might, without losing his respect, let young Tarrenton, who had just come back from a long inspection of his father's interests in Canada, see her as she was now.

As she walked along toward the tank, she remembered how he had looked at her that evening. It seemed that every moment when he hadn't been bringing her something to eat or drink, or dancing with her, he had been looking at her. At thirty he had developed into a splendid young man, with almost red, soft hair, a handsome face and a strong, well set body.

If he could see her now, she giggled, he'd probably do something beyond just stare at her; he'd want to marry her. And Howard Tarrenton was the only man Malou had ever seen that she would have thought of marrying.

Arriving at the edge of the pool, where it was somewhat dark from the trees, Malou found her way out upon the springboard, poised for a moment, gave a bound; curved, thrillingly through the air, and ended in a perfect dive entering the water as cleanly as an arrow.

Under the water she shot through coolness for several feet, and came to the surface, at the shallow end of the tank, squarely into the arms of a man!

"Oh!" said Malou.

"My gunness!" said the man; "you haven't got anything on!"

"I haven't got anything on *you*," she charged, self-possessed in spite of everything.

"I didn't think anyone else would come out here this time of morning," he explained, "otherwise I'd have—but, you see up in Canada, during the warm weather, it's so sparsely settled up there, and the lakes are so secluded that one learns to swim, *au naturel*—it's the swellest way in the world to swim, as evidently you have noticed."

"And how!" Malou agreed. "It's Howard, isn't it?"

"Yes," he said, "it's Howard; and you're Malou Wentworth, aren't you?"

"Now that we know each other," she said, "I suppose I'd better hurry back to the house."

"No," he said, "let *me* go, and you stay here; I've had my swim. You've just come."

"Since we can't see each other," she suggested, "suppose we both stay."

"I was hoping you'd say that," he told her.

"If you'll let me go," she suggested, I'll swim around awhile."

"Oh! I beg your pardon," he said, "I forgot I was holding you." With some difficulty he released his tight grip upon her and she swam away. A moment later he heard a startled:

"Oh! My head!" And then silence. Frantically Howard swam toward the spot where he had heard the startled exclamation. He found her limp in the water near the edge of the pool. Evidently, he decided, she had lost her bearings and swum headlong against the cement side of the pool. He pulled her toward the shallow end, picked her soft wet slippery body up into his arms, carried her out and laid her down upon the edge of the pool.

Not knowing what else to do, he chafed her hands and the rest of her body, supposing that this might possibly stir up some sign of life; but, when nothing happened, he picked her up again and went toward the house. Inside the house, he carried her up to her room; put her down gently upon the bed, turned on the night reading lamp near the bed.

HE HASTILY retreated to his room, slipped into a pair of pajamas and a bathrobe and returned. She still lay perfectly still as he had left her. He racked his brains frantically to think of something to do; but no idea suggested itself except perhaps that a drink of liquor might aid in bringing her to.

He retreated again, hastily, to his room; secured a bottle of whiskey and returned to her side. She had not, so far as he could see, stirred. Putting an arm around behind her he lifted up her head and poured some of the whiskey between her lips. She choked, stirred; sighed, opened her eyes.

"You're in your own room," he said, forestalling her; "I guess you bumped your head against the

She swam away.

cement side of the tank. I'd better go and stir up somebody and get a doctor."

"Oh no, don't," she advised. "I'll be all right; and if you do that, people will wonder and talk about how we happened to be out in the tank together, and how you happened to be in here and everything. That wouldn't do at all!"

"I guess you're right," he admitted, "but what can I do? What treatment do you suggest?"

"You might start by covering me up with something," she suggested reprovingly. "You should have thought of that in the first place."

He blushed and got a cover to throw over her.

"Now what shall I do?" he asked helplessly.

"Stop looking worried," she advised, "and just stay here with me and hold my hand; I feel sort of dizzy, as though I were floating away." She half closed her eyes, and, in a panic, he took her into his arms. He could not have told precisely how it happened; but, at any rate, he found her lips very close to his and kissed them. This seemed to revive her a little so he kissed them again and again, let his mouth dwell upon them. He took her tightly into his arms. She said "Oh!" much as she had when she ran into the concrete.

It was at breakfast the following morning that they met again. [*Continued on page* 66]

Sue: "My boss is an angel."
Prue: "I'm so sorry!"

Exposed to the Law

"Is she out for athletics?"
"No; athletes."

From A Cynic's Notebook

By JOSEPH HUDSON

The girl who forgets herself is generally remembered.

◆◆

It's best to keep light loves in the dark.

◆◆

Men used to become sentimental, and then kiss. Now they kiss first.

◆◆

Working girls are divided into two classes: Those who work somewhere, and those who work someone.

◆◆

Some girls like to be in the dark about their men. Others like to be about their men in the dark.

◆◆

Man depends on his line; woman, on her lines.

F YOU ever saw Kitty Kenyon, you would readily agree that a kiss from her lips was worth any trifling sacrifice. Five feet two of adorable femininity, she was the type of woman that immediately aroused tender desires in the heart of man. There was a delicacy, a charm about her that was not to be denied.

Reginald Smithers, one of her boy friends, was rapidly becoming *the* boy friend. And that, of course, indicates that Reggie was pretty well acquainted with Kitty's kissable lips. They were, indeed, his closest acquaintance! Aside from this, Reggie was a very nice, sedate young fellow —just the type of boy friend that becomes *the*—

It was strange then, that on one hot Summer night when Reggie made his umpty-umpth date with Kitty, she pleaded a headache and broke it—at the very last minute. But Reggie was not the sort of chap that can be put off—as we shall presently discover.

Kitty sat home peacefully reading a magazine, in one of those rare moods for pretty young ladies when men do not matter in the least. Suddenly the doorbell rang.

Wearily she opened the front door.

And in walked Reginald Smithers!

"Darling," he said, in his suave, matter-of-fact way, "I thought I'd just drop in for a little while and help you forget your headache, even if you can't come out with me."

"I've had such a hard day," she said, "and that's why—"

"Then please let me console you by kissing those dear lips of yours," said Reggie, quick to seize an opportunity. But Kitty had jumped up in alarm.

"No! No! Not that! Don't kiss me!"

Reggie looked—and [*Continued on page 64*]

"Now that you've been abroad, do you know any Spanish?"
"Yes, an address book full."

◆◆

"I understand Bill has a charming wife."
"Yes? Who is she charming now?"

◆◆

He: "I'm determined to kiss you before I go home."
She: "Leave this house immediately!"

◆◆

"Marry me?"
"No."
"Aw—just this once!"

Boss: "No, I'm afraid you won't do."
Steno: "Did I say I wouldn't?"

She: "Why did you turn out the light?"
He: "I feel better in the dark."

"Young man! Just WHAT are your intentions?"
"I dunno. I've only been here ten minutes."

◆◆

He: "Are we alone?"
She: "Yes, but I don't feel that way tonight."

◆◆

"I never kiss a girl except on great occasions."
"What do you call great occasions?"
"Whenever I kiss a girl."

◆◆

"Next to your girl, what do you think of most?"
"Next to my girl, I don't think."

AVE TALBOT was filled with ambitions as big as the great open spaces from which he hailed—that is to say, Montana. Out in Pinpoint Junction Dave had gone over with a bang as entertainer at picnics, church socials, rotary banquets, and ladies' night at the local lodges and he therefore picked the stage as a career.

And so, having picked his Complete Magician's Outfit and one spare shirt, Dave came to New York to make his formal debut in vaudeville Wait till the booking agents saw that disappearing Ace-of-spades trick! Wait till they heard a sample of his ventriloquist act! Wait till he pulled that rabbit out of the empty hat!

He took a room at the madhouse known as Lou Belloni's theatrical rooming-house in the West Fifties. The house was filled with practically everything in the world, from trained seals to prima donnas—everything, that is, except money. Among other items it contained Madge Dahl, the hottest, youngest most red-haired and dizzily curved member of that famous trio of sisters known as the Dancing Dahls.

The first time Madge Dahl passed Dave Talbot on the stairs her heart turned a triple somersault and fell over the footlights. Dave was tall and lean and looked as though he had been chiseled from some clean rock in the midst of his vast Montana. His eyes were a remote sea-blue, and his chin was satisfyingly square.

Dave, however, had no eyes for Madge Talbot. Neither on that first day, nor on any of the succeeding days. For Dave was reconnoitering the booking agencies, and no matter how invitingly Madge's brown eyes sparkled Dave could not get his mind away from the sad fact that the vaudeville market seemed to be over-supplied with magicians and ventriloquists—especially inexperienced ones. Dave put in all his spare time at worrying, and practicing up on his repertoire of tricks.

The best act of the lot—or so Dave thought—was his hypnotizing stunt. That was his masterpiece, and he spent endless hours in the privacy of his room rehearsing the magic ritual or reading up on the art in his manual. Dave had offered to prove his worth by demonstrating his mesmeric powers on a dozen different booking agents, but they didn't seem to have the time. And so Dave continued to make mysterious passes in the air.

THEN one peaceful evening as Dave strode the floor of his cubicle muttering the lines of his act, Madge Dahl decided to take matters into her own hands. She happened to be passing Dave's door, and halted in curiosity as his solemn intonation reached her.

"You are now in my power," chanted Dave to himself, waving his hands before the face of an imaginary subject. "Look into my eyes—"

Madge knocked at the door and Dave wonderingly opened it.

"Oh," said Madge in round-eyed curiosity, "are you a hypnotist?"

"Yes, ma'm," admitted Dave politely.

This was a cold beginning, and it sort of pricked Madge's pride. Here she was, five and a fraction feet of adorable, pink-and-white femininity, practically throwing herself into this man's arms, and all he did was placidly admit that he was hypnotist. Madge was distinctly annoyed.

"I don't believe in hypnotism," she flatly declared.

"You don't?" asked Dave amazed.

"Of course not," snapped Madge. "It's just a lot of hokum." That, she decided, ought to put this serious-minded youth in his place.

"Well, it certainly is not," Dave hotly retorted. "It's no more hokum than telephones or the radio. In fact, it's the big stunt in my vaudeville act."

"I'd like to see anybody hypnotize me!" snorted Madge.

"Oh, you would, would you?" rasped Dave defiantly. "Well, just to show you, if you think you're so smart, I will. That is," he taunted her, "if you're game!"

"I'm game all right," announced Madge derisively, and stepped into the room. "On with the trance!"

"Very well, Miss—er—?" said Dave sombrely.

"You can call me Madge," she told him, meltingly, and a trifle nervously. She wondered apprehensively whether there might not be something to this hypnotism business, after all. But of course there wasn't! Let Dave Talbot—she'd learned his name from Lou Belloni—do his best, or worst. She seated herself in a chair, crossing shapely chiffon-clad limbs and glancing insouciantly about the room.

"Go right ahead, Dave," she told him, a sparkle of bold defiance in her brown eyes. "And make it snappy. The Dancing Dahls leave for Buffalo at midnight, starting the Orpheum circuit. Got a clock I can keep my eye on?"

Dave indicated an alarm-clock standing on the dresser. He used it in order to rise promptly at eight o'clock every morning, when the alarm rang, and begin his day's tour of the agencies.

"I'll watch it for you, because you'll be in a trance," he confidently assured her. "Now, Madge, concentrate on looking into my eyes."

Madge did as she was bidden, and found it not particularly difficult. Dave's eye were a deep, steady blue, and his features were dangerously handsome.

"You are now forgetting everything," Dave intoned, making slow motions in the air before Madge's face. "The world is becoming a blank. You cannot remember your name. You feel as though you were on the verge of falling into a deep sleep. You can hardly keep your eyes open, and you are totally unable to move."

Madge's brown eyes indeed took on a surprisingly glassy look, and she seemed almost breathless, sitting without moving a muscle.

"Relax, relax," chanted Dave, continuing his soothing gestures. "You are now in my power. Relax, and breathe deeply."

Madge sank back into the chair with an audible sigh of contentment.

"Look into my eyes," Dave chanted on. "You are now in my power. You have no will-power of your own—"

HE PAUSED long enough to mop his brow over these strenuous exertions, and to consider his handiwork. Madge seemed as though she were made of wax. Dave, in all his experience at hypnotism out in Pinpoint Junction, had never seen anyone in quite so profound a trance. It almost frightened him, she sat so still and speechless. And her eyes stared at him with a peculiar intentness Dave found quite disconcerting.

He wondered nervously what happened to a person who was too thoroughly hypnotized. He rose and searched feverishly for his Manual of Mesmerism. He found it, at last, in the bathroom,

where he had been perusing it the evening before while enjoying a hot bath. A hasty reading of the handbook reassured him. A deep trance might last several hours, but the subject always came out of it, in the end.

Dave returned to Madge and considered her with triumph in his eye. It was the most perfect job of hypnotism he had ever performed. Just to test out his powers, Dave decided to put the subject through a few simple manoeuvres.

"Rise," he peremptorily commanded Madge.

Madge obediently rose, like one moving in her sleep.

Dave regarded her with satisfaction. Truly, he had complete sway over her. She hadn't a thought in the world outside of those he put into her head.

"Come here," commanded Dave, vaguely thrilled at his power.

Madge advanced till she stood almost in his arms, her cute red hair shining just under his chin, her body glowing and fragrant. All at once Dave was filled with a wayward impulse.

"Kiss me," he softly commanded.

Madge obediently tilted her face up to his, her scarlet oval of a mouth puckered expectantly. She rose on tip-toe and pressed her satiny lips to Dave's in a lingering, vibrant kiss. Somehow, Dave's wayward impulse grew stronger, and he returned the kiss with interest.

"Put your arms around me," he ordered her.

Madge obediently raised her arms, slipped them about his shoulders, and clung to him in a radiant, submissive heap. Before he knew what he was doing Dave had seized her in his own arms and was hungrily embracing the warm contours of her yielding form. Several breathless moments passed thus, and then Dave reluctantly released her. He surveyed her as she stood obediently before him in her clinging gown that revealed a thousand kissable curves, and wild thrills began to chase up and down his spine.

"Now," said Dave in a vibrant whisper, "take off your dress."

He didn't really think that she would. Somehow it didn't seem possible that he had complete sway over this gorgeous creature. The words just sort of popped out of his mouth of their own accord.

But Madge gave instant obedience, while Dave watched with incredulous delight. She gave the

"Kiss me," he commanded.

gown a business-like yank and peeled it up over the dizzy perfections of a slender, girlishly lithe and vital body, pulled it over her head, and dropped the garment on the floor beside her, her flaming red hair falling askew over shining eyes and cheeks.

Clad in a pink chemise filmy as the foam of Champagne, and about as big as a postage stamp, she was a sight that set Dave's pulse to racing and made him swallow very hard.

She looked at him through lustrous brown eyes, her tiny lips parted in a faint smile.

For a moment Dave suffered the twinges of a stern conscience. Was he doing quite right, he wondered, in using his extraordinary power in this audacious way? But then he quieted his conscience by recalling the way she had twitted him about hypnotism. Hokum, she had called it. And now look at her, absolutely at his mercy! It served her right, thought Dave. And besides, the male in him was aroused to the point where it was strong enough to throttle several consciences.

"Come here," he commanded Madge once more.

Madge came to him, her high-heeled slippers making sharp little clicks on the floor. She walked straight up to him. Slowly, but hungrily, Dave slipped his arms about her velvety form, his lips straying over the rich softness of her lips and cheeks.

"Kiss me again," Dave commanded her huskily, "and again!"

Madge's lips pressed against his in eager obedience, like two tiny flames. Her arms went about his neck again in a strangling embrace. Her eyes slid gently shut, and her breath came in quick little gasps.

Dave lifted her suddenly into his arms, and gazed adoringly down at her. What a trance she was in! Truly, his Manual of Mesmerism did not exaggerate the strange powers of the successful hypnotist. Madge clung to him meltingly as though content to remain in his arms forever, her face without a single wrinkle of alarm or protest. Instead, her berry-red lips and flushed, shining cheeks expressed nothing but sheer, trance-like bliss. She seemed incapable of any thoughts except those planted in her mind by Dave. To those, she was more than acquiescent.

Dave bore her across the room and deposited her gently on a chair.

"Say 'I love you,'" commanded Dave masterfully.

"I love you," murmured Madge in a quivering, obedient whisper.

Dave pressed savage, fiery kisses upon her demurely smiling lips—

Dave was distracted, some moments later, by the ringing of his alarm clock. Puzzled, Dave stepped to the dresser and shut off the alarm, noting that it was just twelve o'clock. That was odd. He hadn't set the alarm for that hour.

Dave turned back to Madge, remembering that she was scheduled to leave for Buffalo. He'd have to bring her out of her trance, and do it in a hurry. But to his surprise, Madge was already sitting up, matter-of-factly tucking her hair into place and reaching for her clothes.

"Wait," commanded Dave, "I've got to bring you out of your coma."

"I haven't got time, Dave," said Madge in a business-like tone, flashing him, nevertheless, a dazzling smile. [*Continued on page* 61]

By TRIXIE WOLF

Dear Miss Wolf:

What would you think of a boy who gave you silk underwear and then insisted on seeing you in it?

INSULTED.

DEAR INSULTED:

I'd say he was a smart lad!

Dear Trixie:

I am a young girl of sixteen and have recently discovered that the boys go wild over me. I bobbed my hair last year, and this year I am going in for the tricky little things that the older girls wear to entice the men . . . silk stockings, teddies, etc. However, I am at a loss to understand one thing. Why is it that every time I go riding with a fellow, he insists upon turning off the main road and finding a deserted lane in the woods? Last week I was stuck in the mud twice.

SIXTEEN.

DEAR SIXTEEN:

Look out or you'll get stuck with a husband!

Dear Miss Wolf:

You seem to know just about everything. I wonder if you could tell me a good way to make punch for thirty couples. I'm having a brawl (I mean ball) at a lake resort and want to find a way to get everyone feeling good at little expense.

HOSTESS.

DEAR HOSTESS:

Take a gallon of alky and mix it with a case of Canada Dry gingerale, and add a quart of grape juice and a big hunk of ice. And how about inviting me to the party?

Dear Miss Wolf:

I am a young man of seventeen and can't seem to get anywhere with the girls. Of course I suppose you'd rather answer questions of flappers, but thought I'd take a chance.

TOM.

DEAR TOM:

If you don't take a chance once in a while, you'll die a lonely man. You say you can't seem to get anywhere with the girls. Just *where* do you want to get? Tell *me* and I'll tell *you!*

Dear Trix:

Well, old girl, how is your wooden leg? I see by SNAPPY that you hand out a mean line of red hot advice to flappers. Well, I'm no flapper, but without me the flappers would be mighty hard up . . . for I'm the answer to a flapper's prayer. Tall, blonde, strong, passionate, plenty of money, a Packard . . . and lots of that old Sex Appeal. Could you find me a girl?

HOT SHOT HARRY.

DEAR HOT SHOT HARRY:

Just a minute big boy! What are you trying to do, kid an old lady like me? If you're as smooth as you say, why ask me how to get a girl? I think you're off your coco, if you'll pardon the French! And I haven't a wooden leg!

Dear Miss Wolf:

You seem to hit the nail right on the head. What would you do if your fellow never took you out or bought you anything?

BESS.

DEAR BESS:

I'd hit HIM right on the head!

Dear Trixie:

Do you think a girl can get ahead in New York if she has her own apartment, and throws a big party once in a while for a gang of gorillas? I happen to know a couple of gunmen who have lots of *what it takes*, and they want me to give parties for their boy friends. Do you think I would get shot?

CHICAGO BELLE.

DEAR CHICAGO BELLE:

You might do very well being the moll of a dozen gangsters . . . it seems that the moll of ONE gangster gets along pretty soft, as the saying goes. As for your getting shot, the chances are you'll get at least half shot. Let me know how the party comes out, but be sure to have them check their machine guns in the hall . . . and watch those black jacks!

P. S. Better wear bullet-proof step-ins!

Dear Miss Wolf:

I am so in love with a boy that I can't eat, or sleep, or talk, or think. He wants me to take a trip with him on his yacht, but he can't marry me as he has another wife. What would you do?

HEARTBURN.

DEAR HEARTBURN:

You certainly have a problem. If you don't eat or sleep or talk or think, I can't see why he couldn't afford to keep you around while his wife isn't looking. It's the *eating* and *talking* that bother married men. The *thinking* they don't mind . . . and of course they are simply WILD about a girl who can't sleep! He might throw his wife overboard!

Never Say Dice!

APRIL WALLICE was being kissed again —for perhaps the thousandth time. On this occasion the man in the case was Jimmie MacAleer, the artist.

April enjoyed being kissed, purely as a study in masculine psychology. She liked to compare the reactions of the various men to whom she surrendered her delicious, bee-stung lips. A few—a very few—kissed her gravely and politely and were duly thankful; but these were in the minority, and mostly past the first flush of youth. Most men, kissing April, lost their heads in the intoxication of the moment. In such a class was Jimmie MacAleer.

April, clinging close to him, could feel his body vibrate as his lips found and pressed hers.

Like a hungering animal, he crushed her close to him. April abruptly found herself smothering, gasping for breath under the impetuous ardor of his love-making.

With a little laugh, she pushed him away. "That's all there is, Jimmie—there isn't any more!" she said with finality.

He stared at her, his eyes narrowed and gleaming. They were on the terrace of a very famous and very surreptitious gambling estate on Long Island—a place where the elite of four states congregated when they wanted to tempt the goddess of fortune for high stakes. In fact, someone had dubbed it the secret Monte Carlo of America—and it was just an hour's drive from the heart of New York.

Through the filtered moonbeams on the terrace, Jimmie MacAleer stared at April, and breathed hard. "You—you mean you were just—teasing me?" he demanded heavily.

April very calmly powdered her nose in the moonlight and laughed again. "Surely you didn't think me serious, Jimmie?" she gibed. She watched him out of the corner of her eye—watched him as a chemist might watch an experimental test-tube heated by a Bunsen burner. Only it was plain to be seen that Jimmie needed no Bunsen burner at that instant!

Jimmie turned on his heel. "I'm going in to get a drink!" he said shortly.

April smiled. So many men, after they had kissed April, went and got drunk! She caught up with him and grabbed his arm. "I'll go in too," she said. "I've got just one hundred-dollar bill left. I'm going to play it on the red. If I lose, you'll take me right home, won't you Jimmie?"

He shook her hand from his elbow. "I suppose I'll have to—I brought you here!" he growled.

They re-entered the secret casino. Gambling—and experimenting with men—were April Wallice's two greatest thrills. She approached a rou-

If You Do You May Find Yourself In The Same Predicament

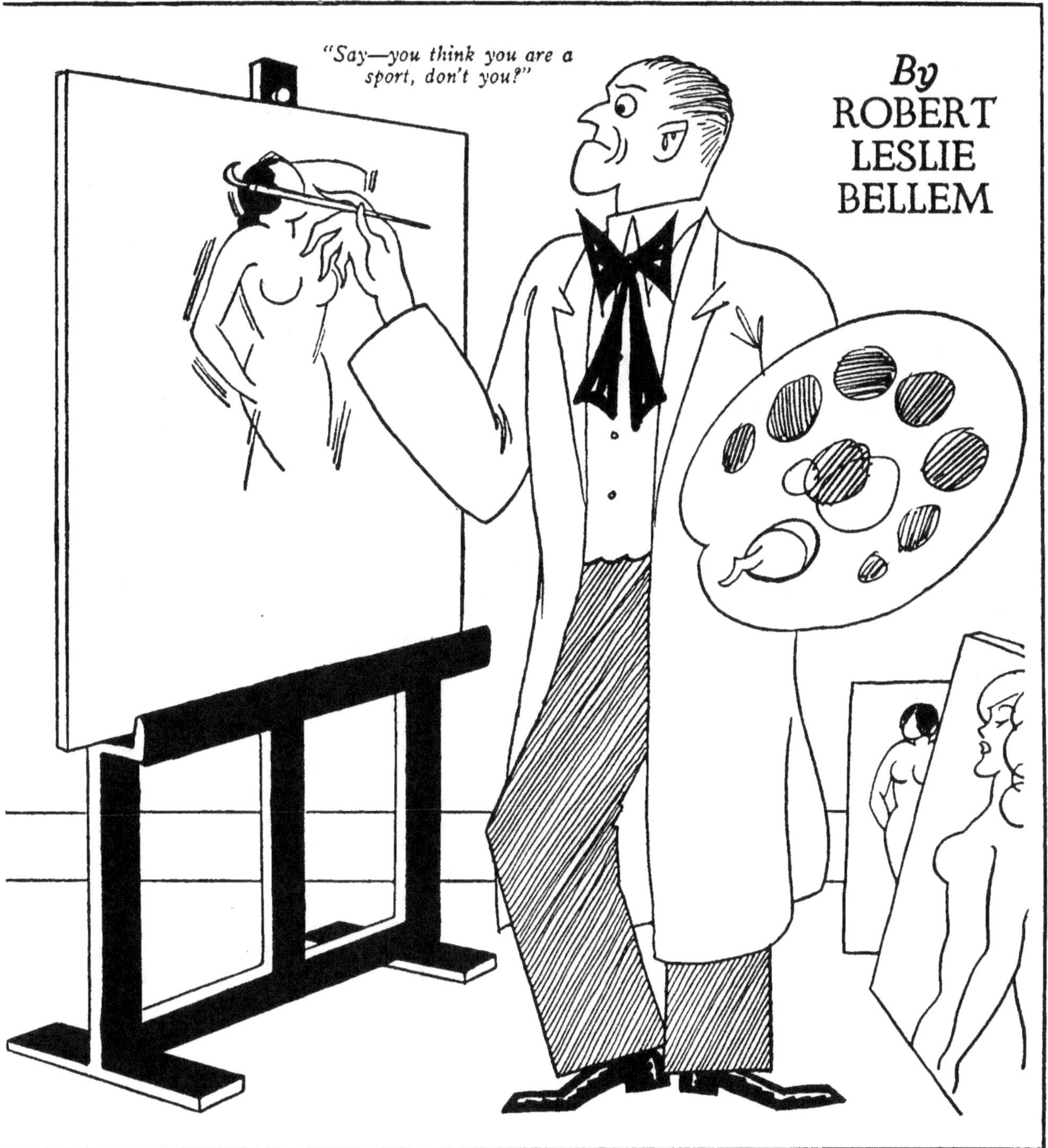

lette table and watched the croupier turn the wheel and send the little ivory ball spinning around its groove. With a nonchalant gesture she tossed her last hundred dollars on the red.

The little ball fell from its track, bounced against the revolving wheel four times, and settled —into a black number.

April made a little face. "That's that!" she remarked, and turned from the table. "I'm ready to go home, Jimmie."

In his car he drove silently, sullenly for nearly a half-hour. Then he faced her suddenly. "Look here, April—was that your last money?" he demanded.

She nodded brightly. "Yes. But what of it?" I'll be getting my usual quarterly remittance from my dear departed uncle's estate in a few days. I'll manage. My rent's paid, thank heavens."

He slowed the car to a snail's pace. "Listen, April, you little yellow-haired imp from hell! If

As April Wallice Does in This Gayly Diverting Little Story

I can't persuade you to pose for me out of—well, call it friendship—perhaps I can sell you on the idea commercially. I'll give you five hundred dollars if you'll let me put you on canvas!"

She laughed her tinkling, mellow laugh. "My dear Jimmie, I shall never appear in the nude for any man except my husband—if I ever get one. And considering the fun I'm having as a single young lady, I don't think I'll ever have a husband. Ergo, I'll never appear in the nude."

He stepped hard on the accelerator, and then slowed down again. "You listen to me, April Wallice! I'm desperate. I can't sleep. I can't eat, I can't paint, until I've had a chance to paint *you.* If you're going to be so damned obstinate about it, I'll paint you with clothes on. But I've *got* to paint you!"

SHE snuggled closer to him, so that her warm young body sent an electric thrill coursing through his spine. "Is it as bad as that, Jimmie?" she whispered.

He nodded glumly.

"Then—I'll do it!" she said softly. He straightened up and almost swerved the car into the ditch. She touched his arm. "On one condition," she stipulated, and there was a hard, mischievous ring in her voice.

"Name your condition!" he answered swiftly. "It's worth it—anything—if you'll pose for me."

"Well," she said, "if I pose for you you must agree *never to kiss me again!*"

She watched him—watched the muscles of his face and neck working angrily. "The question is, which do you want more? The possibility of my kisses, or—the chance to put me on canvas?"

He stared at her. "You're serious? You'd make it that tough for me to decide?"

She nodded.

He hesitated. Then he burst out. "Be at my studio at nine tomorrow morning!" he stormed. "Damn your kisses! I'll paint you, and then maybe I can get some sleep!"

She drew over to her own corner of the seat. "Perhaps you've decided wisely," she answered judicially. "At least, if you manage to get some sleep, perhaps you can dream about my vanished kisses!" And she giggled fiendishly.

He braked the car in front of her apartment and helped her out. She gave him her cool, smooth hand. "Thanks for a wonderful evening, Jimmie," she said. "Good night—and I'll see you at your studio at nine in the morning. Shall I wear a simple frock, or a formal gown?"

"Make it a formal gown—and the lower the *decolletage,* the better!" he muttered.

She laughed. "Formal it shall be. Good night, Jimmie."

He faced her. "Aren't you going to kiss me goodnight?"

She shook her head and smiled. "A bargain's a bargain, Jimmie!" she reproved him, and vanished inside the apartment house.

Punctually at nine the following morning, April Wallice drew up in a taxi before Jimmie MacAleer's studio in Greenwich Village. She swept out of the vehicle, resplendent in high-heeled evening slippers and ermine wrap. The driver grinned, as much as to say, "You've been out all night, young lady, and I know it!"

April eyed him coldly. "Wait here!" she commanded, and ran up the flight of stairs to Jimmie's studio, her rounded calves flashing silkily. MacAleer was waiting for her. She grinned. "Go down and pay my taxi-man; I'm flat!" she said imperiously.

While he was gone, she shrugged out of the ermine wrap, slipped in front of a big mirror, and arranged her appearance to her own satisfaction. Her ash-blonde hair was regally coiffed; her bee-stung lips just sufficiently encarmined; her eyes kohled so artistically as to defy detection. Her neck, her shoulders, her throat, her peach-bloom, satiny skin all pleased her. She smiled faintly to herself. Jimmie MacAleer needn't know that she'd sat up until dawn, making the *decolletage* more daring, more revelatory, on the gown she wore. She almost blushed as she realized how much of her she was actually revealing!

The artist came bounding into the studio. He surveyed her critically. Then he smiled. "Lord, you're beautiful, April!" he said earnestly. "I'll make you my masterpiece!"

"I may be your masterpiece, but you won't make me, Jimmie!" she grinned.

He frowned savagely. "Don't worry. You needn't flaunt your virtue at me so early in the morning. As far as I'm concerned, from now on you're just a model—an object I intend to reproduce on canvas. Stand over there on that platform. Now sit on that chair. That's it. I like that pose."

HE STUDIED her. "Can't you let that dress come a little lower in front?" he asked suddenly.

She blushed a tiny blush. "Not without disastrous consequences," she answered.

He approached her. "April, why are you so damned modest? Don't you realize that a body as beautiful as yours belongs to the world of art? You're selfish! Why can't you be a sport and pose for me the way you should pose—in the nude?"

"I haven't really lost yet," she said.

"What's being a sport got to do with it?" she challenged him.

He seemed struck with a sudden idea. "Say—you think you *are* a sport, don't you? You think you're a big-time gambler, just because you risk an occasional hundred dollars or so? I wonder," he achieved a sneer, "how much of a gambler you'd be if something a lot more personal than money were up as a stake?"

"What do you mean?" she asked sharply. "Nobody ever caught me welching yet!"

He went to a desk and came back with a pair of dice in his hand. "Suppose I made a proposition to you? Suppose I suggested that we throw dice to see how much—or how little—clothing you wear when you pose for me?"

She was silent for a moment, mulling over the idea. Then she laughed, and as usual, there was mischief in her laughter. "I'd take you up—if the gamble weren't all in your favor."

"What do you mean?"

"I mean that the way you've suggested the game, you've got everything to gain and nothing to lose. Suppose we play this way: if I win, I wear my ermine wrap over this dress—and if I win twice, I wear it high around my throat. If I lose, of course—well—"

"It's a bet!" he cried. He handed her one of the dice. "Shoot high dice to see who gets the cubes first!" he said excitedly.

A gambler's flush mounted to April's cheeks. She accepted the die and flung it to the floor. It rolled up a four!

Jimmie MacAleer threw his single die down. It showed three! "Your dice!" he said to April.

She picked up the cubes, rattled them, blew on them and let them hit the platform. "Six-five!" she yelled. "I wear the ermine wrap!" She

"You may look at the picture now," he said.

picked up the dice and rattled them again. "Now to see if I close it at the throat!" she crooned. She flung the cubes from her. Two aces showed. "Craps!" Jimmie MacAleer shouted. "There goes your ermine wrap!"

"Still my dice!" she informed him. She shook the ivory squares and rolled them out. "Six-three! Little Nina! Come to mama! Let's go!" She threw the dice again—and turned pale. A six and an ace gleamed at her.

"You fell off!" MacAleer said with satisfaction. He picked up the dice and rubbed them behind his back for luck. "Now we'll see what's what!" he breathed grimly. He threw the cubes on the floor. "Seven!" he exclaimed. "There goes your dress!"

"I've still got my step-ins and a brassiere, not to mention shoes and stockings!" April said tardy.

He threw the cubes again. "Eleven!" he yelled. "There's your boasted brassiere! Off with it!"

April hesitated the barest fraction of a second. He grinned. "You never welch, eh?"

She tossed her head. "No, I never do!" she retorted, and pulled the low-cut gown off over her blonde head. Then, with a swift snap, she unfastened the brassiere where it was snapped behind her, and—shrugged out of it!

April stood there regally, like some queen enslaved. Her rounded shoulders melted into a perfect chest; her flat, muscular torso was revealed in all its purity.

Jimmie MacAleer didn't even look. He was rattling the dice. He threw them. "Seven again!" he shouted. "That's shoes and stockings!"

April grimly leaned over and divested herself of sheer hose and high-heeled pumps. There was nothing left now between April and complete revealment save the thin, lacy step-in.

The artist picked up the dice and heaved them one more time. "A natural—eleven!" he whooped. "Hand me that step-in!"

April turned pink all over—a fact which was plainly to be seen. But she was game. Her unclad body shuddered just a little as her fingers went falteringly toward the step-in's waistband around her flat little stomach. She fumbled with it—at last succeeded in unfastening it. A sudden wave of modesty overcame her. She turned her back on Jimmie MacAleer as the step-in fluttered to the floor.

He gazed with professional approval at the flat curves of her—the willowy, simple slenderness of her hips, the rounded, athletic lilt of her calves and thighs. "Turn around!" he commanded.

Like a frightened wood-nymph she turned and faced him.

He came close to her. She shrank away—and then steeled herself. He was a stranger; he was no longer the Jimmie MacAleer she knew. He was a robot, an automaton. There was something strictly impersonal in the way he touched her here and there, guided her lithe, responsive body into he pose he desired. His very indifference, his detachment, seemed to steady her. She relaxed, grew more at ease—and in the instant of relaxation, achieved the pose he wanted.

"Fine! Hold it!" he exclaimed, and dashed for his easel and canvas.

For three weeks April came to Jimmie's studio, Sundays included. Twenty-one days she came, divested herself of every stitch of raiment, and posed at Jimmie MacAleer's bidding. And on the twenty-second day, he [*Continued on page 64*]

Dumb Dora thinks that lettuce is a proposition.

◆◆

He: "Well, you don't dance, drink or smoke?"
She: "Oh, no, sir."
He: "I'm coming right over. You must do something!"

◆◆

"Listen kid, what's to prevent us from having a real wild time tonight?"
"Oh, my goodness!"

She: "How do I look, dear?"
He: "Sweet enough to kiss."
She: "Aw—go on."

◆◆

"I see where two girls walked from San Francisco to Denver."
"They should have got out of the car sooner."

◆◆

"You say you went out riding with Tom last night? How did you get home?"
"Road."

◆◆

Jane: "I wonder if he loves me."
June: "Sure! Why should he make an exception of you?"

Roger Made Up His Mind to Find Her, if It Took the Rest of His Life—and See What Happened

T WAS a quiet evening in late August. At ten thirty Forty-Eighth Street near Sixth was as peaceful as a country lane. Half way down the block Roger Ashley, in his parked Hispano, was waiting for a friend.

Time passed. It was now ten thirty-one. Without a second's notice, the quiet burst into complete eruption. Crashes. The brave sound of axes splintering wood and glass. The screams and shouts of infuriated bartenders, indignant ladies, and cynical police.

Roger sat up. Out of the old-fashioned mansion whence the crashes were issuing, a slight girlish figure came running. She darted up the street, across the sidewalk and, jerking open the door of Roger's car tumbled into the seat next to him.

"Whirl the old propeller, stranger," bade a charming voice, "and see if we can make Boston or hell in two hours."

Roger stared. He saw long blue eyes burning in a fresh oval face. He saw a tender mouth savage with paint.

Roger smiled. This was a lot nicer than meeting Jack Williams and talking over old college days. He stepped on the gas just as a blue clad figure came out of the house and started to yell "Hey, stop!"

"I hit him with a bottle of real rye," explained the girl regretfully as the car zoomed up Sixth and into the Park. It was nice and cool and dark. Roger glided the car into a lonely spot near the lake and stopped.

"I love nature," he said, expertly slipping his arm around a soft waist.

The girl laughed gently. "I really prefer this sort of thing under a roof," she said. "But if you must have a kiss, close your eyes and I'll surprise you."

Roger closed his eyes. The next moment he was clutching empty air instead of the soft curves he anticipated fondling. From a nearby bush came a low mocking laugh. Roger sprang out. He searched long and well. He might as well have been looking for a needle in a haystack, a colored gent in a pile of coal or what have you? He returned to the car cursing under his breath. He went home.

It is the songs we can't sing that start us warbling. It is the kisses that have eluded us that start us dreaming. Roger's dreams that night were full of the burning-eyed, slim-thighed maiden whose lips had not quite met his. He told himself it was nonsense, but he couldn't forget her. He swore to himself that if it took the rest of his natural life he would find her. No girl had ever played that one on him. If he ever encountered her again—his breath came fast at the thought of how he would crush her under his kisses.

Yes, snappy reader, as you have doubtless suspected, it was a case of love at first sight for Roger. But what was he going to do about it? He didn't know her name. He didn't know her address. He knew nothing but that the light of her eyes and the momentary vision he had had of the region above the stocking-line had set up a tumult in his brain.

Three days later he still felt tumultuous. He sulked in his pent-house. He refused invitations to bridge and strip-poker parties. Being a young man with plenty of leisure, he had little to do but worry over the miss he had just missed kissing. He drove the Hispano up and down Forty-Eighth as if luck could again bring him a speak-easy raid and a bolt from such blue eyes. Central Park, too, saw a lot of his four wheels. He fell into a deep melancholy. What availed it to be young, fairly handsome, with a dandy pent-house where love's mysteries could be made certainties far above the city's roar, if one couldn't explore them with the one girl?

He was thinking of going to Alaska or the Fiji Isles for distraction when Lola breezed in.

"I want ten bucks from you, old dear," she said. "That's your fee for the treasure hunt."

"Me no sabe," said Roger.

"It's for the benefit of the Indigent Armenian Committee," explained Lola. "Saturday night you will get an envelope containing the first clue. You follow that and you'll get a second. By the end of the evening, you'll find the pot of gold at the rainbow's end, if someone doesn't get there ahead of you."

Roger paid his ten and got a hearty kiss. It

She sat down on the floor and began to cry.

didn't interest him. As we have remarked before, nothing interested him but the kiss he had just failed to take that thrilling night of the raid.

By Saturday he had almost forgotten about the treasure-hunt for the Armenians when his valet appeared bearing a small envelope on a tray.

"This just arrived by messenger, sir," he said.

Listlessly Roger tore open the envelope. It contained a slip of paper on which was typed:

HKOVMDOZPQL DUCJEKD

It teased him, this brainless message from he knew not whom. Knowing something of cryptograms, he found himself working on this one. When he had deciphered it, it said:

MASTERBUILT DOORMAN

Darn clever, these Armenians! In much need of any distraction Roger took his hat, saddled his Hispano, and five minutes later he was in deep converse with the doorman of the newly opened Masterbuilt Hotel.

"Have you a clue or something for me?" said Roger.

"Oh, yes, sir, yes indeed," said the doorman.

He handed Roger another envelope. The insert said, plainly and temptingly:

Go to room 912.

She smiled, a bit timorously.

Roger went. What else was there for a gloomy young man to do?

He knocked at the door. The sound of a piano accompanying a soprano voice suddenly ceased, and the voice said, "Come right in, the door's open."

Roger walked in. This wasn't a bad sort of game, this treasure-hunt. And he was confirmed in his sentiment when he saw the lady who had asked him to enter.

She was a platinum-haired blonde, the girl sitting at the piano of that exquisitely appointed drawing-room. One was struck by her hair the moment one saw her. But Roger did not look at her hair. For she was wearing a negligee of sleazy black that revealed every line of her figure and judging from the glimpses of ivory flesh behind it, it was the only garment she wore.

"I beg your pardon," said Roger like the gentleman he was, "I hope I am not intruding."

"If you're the gentleman who's in a treasure-hunt or something, you're quite welcome," she said. Smiling, she rose and coming towards him, drew a little envelope from her bosom.

"Oh, this is the next clue, is it?" asked Roger, somewhat dazed.

"Yes, indeed." Suddenly she appeared aware of his gaze. "Please pardon my costume," she said, "but it's so awfully warm to-night."

An exquisite, subtle perfume came from her person. It seemed to breathe of warm, exotic kisses, of lithe ecstasies. And her eyes, too, had an unmistakable come hither look.

"Won't you stay a moment before you hop off to your next clue," she invited. "I'll sing a song or two for you if you'd care to listen."

But Roger was suddenly moody again. What, after all, did he care for the mature charms of this soprano? In his mind was an image of a slender girl, with burning blue eyes, with a body slender as a willow. If he couldn't meet her, what did he care for any other gifts of fate?

"I'm sorry," he said politely, "but if I don't hurry some other chap will win the treasure. Thank you and good-bye!"

She tossed her head. "Oh, very well!" and turning her shapely back on him, walked away. He made his exit.

Outside he wiped his brow.

"Whoever arranged this treasure-hunt did a good night's work," he commented and tore open the envelope still redolent of the perfume of Miss Soprano's bosom.

Fifty-Seventh Street Towers—14 G. Ring 5.

"On with the hunt!" cried Roger and, mounting his trusty Hispano again he wafted himself to the Towers, was shot up to the fourteenth floor and, wondering if what was going to be would be as nice as what had been, rang the bell, five times as per directions.

For a moment nothing happened. Then slowly the door began to open. Roger stared. It was creepy.

There certainly was no one behind that door. But he was not the sort of man who can be daunted by mysteries. Taking a deep breath he marched in.

The door, again without the aid of human hands, slowly began to close.

"Is that you?" called a girl's voice from somewhere in the interior.

"It's me," replied Roger, for who else was it after all?

"Then come into the bar and have a drink."

Roger followed the voice through a corridor on which gave several very sumptuously furnished rooms, as he saw from a hasty glimpse. One, a bedroom, in which a pink light glowed, was especially tempting to the eye and expectation, with the daintiest of beds whose lace cover was charmingly and pointedly turned down.

"Well, all things come to him who goes treasure-hunting in this mad metropolis," murmured Roger to himself, and going three or five steps further, he found himself at the entrance of what undoubtedly was a revival engagement of an old-fashioned bar.

"Oh!" said Roger.

Now he wasn't naif enough to utter an exclamation at the sight of good old-fashioned mahogany, brass rail and bottles of liquor. He had seen such before in the very best of houses. But the girl who stood with one bare foot on the rail, holding a glass of brown stuff in one hand, was dressed in just a single garment that eclipsed even Miss Soprano's in frankness. She wore a pink chemise.

"The Arabian nights had nothing on this!" murmured Roger.

"Did you say something?" asked the girl.

"I said, how did I get here?" said Roger.

"Oh, I work the door with an electric contraption. Saves so much time when the servants are all out. They are all out to-night, you know," she confided.

"How nice."

"So I'm doing a lil' solitary drinking in my private bar. Don't min' my costume. It's fearfully hot out, isn't it? Will you have a drink?"

"I'll have a clue," said Roger.

"Clue, clue?" She seemed to rack her brains while Roger's quick eyes shot over her.

She was a beauty. Her throat was like ivory.

"Oh, yes, I remember—you're one of the treasure-hunters. Come on, have a drink." Suddenly she sat down on the floor and began to cry. "I'm all alone in the world to-night and I'm so lonesome. Oh, nice boy, take pity on me and stay a while or as long as you like!"

Roger went over and picked her up. For a moment she collapsed against him. Softly every curve of her body seemed to melt against him. And the odor of liquor from her parted lips only added to the madness that seized Roger.

Well, he didn't even kiss her. Believe it or not, this is the truth. For again the image of the young beauty whom he was never to see again floated before his eyes and before that image even the real charms before him were powerless.

This was too much. Roger strode in.

He shook his lovely entertainer.

"Be yourself," he bade. "Where is my clue?"

"On the table near the door as you go out," she said crossly. She looked at him with pleading.

Roger marched out. He heard a soft sigh behind him, but he did not even turn. He found an envelope on the table as directed and, pulling open the door, hastened to the elevator.

"If it gets any better than this, I'll sure lose whatever amateur standing I've got," he told himself. "Haven't the girls of Manhattan anything better to do to-night than play Lorelei in pink chemises? We'll see."

The soprano, the bartender, the pint-sized brunette.

But the next *was* better. The clue read, "Eleven Harrow Studio Party. Ask every girl till clue."

And speeding his charger to the Village, pumping up two flights of stairs, pounding on a door behind which came the most weird racket of voices and music he had ever heard, Roger found himself in the midst of the maddest party he had ever attended.

There were about two dozen people in the big square room with its grand north windows. And every one, man or boy, girl or woman, was in some state of undress. A phonograph was playing madly, the air was full of smoke, and in the center of the room a number of the oddly attired couples were dancing.

"Whoopsie!" cried a pint-sized brunette as she attached herself to Roger. It was such a good attachment that he had to actually struggle before she removed her lips and her half-nude body from his.

"What is this?" asked Roger.

"A strip-drink party!" she explained. "Every drink you take in, you take off another article of clothes. I've had six drinks and I'm going to drink myself stark!" she said proudly.

"Good!" said Roger, "but I'm looking for a clue."

He really balked at the idea of going through the crowd and asking every one of these Nudities of Thirty-One for the clue and so was delighted when she pointed to her left leg and said, "If you want it, take it!"

Roger bent down and removed the little envelope from her stocking. Then, nobly declining her invitation to see if there wasn't another clue in the other stocking, he turned and made his way into the night. [*Continued on page 66*]

The Mice Will Play, as the Old Proverb Says, and So—

CHARACTERS:
He
She

SCENE: *A hotel room in New York. Elaborately furnished. In the center, a tray full of good things in bottles.*

HE: (*Entering.*) Are you sure you'll be alone?

SHE: You bet.

HE: Great. And there's no chance of—of—

SHE: Of his coming in? Of course not, silly. Care for a drink?

HE: (*Taking one.*) Sure. We'll have a jolly time, won't we?

SHE: (*Teasing.*) When the cat's away, the mice will play!

HE: And how! Gee, this liquor is great. And what do you say to a little kiss, eh, honey?

SHE: All right. But my conscience hurts. After all, John wouldn't like it and—

HE: John! John! Always John! What did you want to marry a man for if—

SHE: Hush! It isn't fair of us. Well, here's mud in your eye! (*Taking another drink.*) Let's hope John never finds out about this little meeting of ours.

HE: I don't care if he does find out!

SHE: What! Think of the scandal! Think of the—

HE: To heck with it! *Just because your brother is staying with you and he's a prohibition agent, is no reason why I can't have a quiet little drink with my wife if I want to!*

CURTAIN

HONORS *EVEN*

ALWAYS on the lookout for feminine youth and beauty, Paul Mordaunt was struck speechless with appreciation when he saw the girl at the table a short way from his own.

A competent judge, he was sure that she was between eighteen and nineteen. For a moment she glanced his way, and he got an electric flash from large, dazzling black eyes, fringed with long silky lashes that came down over them bashfully at his ardent gaze.

She must be, he judged, some daughter of the bourgeoise out for a wild evening with her shipping clerk beau. Knowing something of women's clothes, he was sure that what she wore did not represent an expenditure of over forty dollars net. When she rose to dance, he was still further impressed.

She was a trifle taller than he had expected she would be, and lithe as a young willow tree swayed in the wind. Her mouth was small, but full and perfect; her lips were damp from the wine her escort had bought her. Paul shivered in ecstasy as he thought of capturing those girl lips with his.

When her escort left the table for a moment, Paul sent over his card. He was delighted when he saw the girl, after a bright glance at him, borrow a pencil from the waiter and scribble something on the card. She penciled briefly: "Thomasine," and a telephone number, Paul saw, when the waiter returned his card. Paul nodded his comprehension before the return of her escort.

"You'll have dinner with me again tomorrow night," he said, anxiously.

Paying his bill he rose and started for the door. The girl's escort was seated with his back toward Paul. Passing very near the table, Paul looked down, from the height of his nearly six feet, at her.

She was probably a stenographer, out with a cheap escort. She had looked at the handsome stranger who so boldly sent her his card and decided that she would take a chance. Paul was extremely glad that he was youthful looking, at forty; his friends told him he looked thirty-five. True, his hair was graying a bit at temples, but, to a young girl, this only provided an added thrill.

Handsome, slim, erect, faultlessly clad, with liquid brown eyes that had made things easy for him with a great many women, Paul had every right to be confident; especially since his attire, his bearing, everything, defined him as a man of means and, as Thomasine would doubtless put it, "Class."

No wonder, accustomed perhaps only to the society of shipping clerks and soda jerkers, she had snatched at the opportunity to make a real conquest. In New York, Paul well enough knew, plenty of girls were that way—and not bad girls either.

Times were changing, and the day when an intelligent, good-looking girl would pass up obvious

Paul Finds the Prize Beauty of Them All

By HOWARD KENNEDY

opportunities for tenuous conventional reasons was long since past.

At six o'clock the following evening, Paul called the number on the card. A woman whose accent and manner of speaking indicated her as certainly no gentlewoman answered the phone.

"'Thomasine?'" she repeated, "Yes, just a moment."

Presently Paul heard an exquisitely soft and girlish voice over the 'phone. He did not mince matters.

"I am the man who sent you his card last night, at the night club," he explained. "As you know from my card, I am Paul Mordaunt, the theatrical manager. I frequent such places as the one you found me in last night, in search of fresh young beauty for my enterprises. You interested me. Would you care to drop around? I'll see that you get a bite of supper here, and then we can talk things over."

"I'll come right now," she said excitedly. Paul

told her to take a cab and have the apartment doorman tell the driver to collect at the desk.

When he had hung up the receiver, Paul paced the floor in deep enthusiasm. It was partly true that he was interested in her professionally. One of the newer producers to compete in revue circles, he managed to make a nice return on his investment through abandoning everything faintly connected with real ability in the theatre, and loading his stage, simply, with pounds of pulchritude as nearly undraped as possible.

Though independently well off, the theatrical business appealed to him for more reasons than one. Thomasine, he realized, was his greatest find so far. In all his looking, since he had been producing shows, he had never seen anything to compare with her.

HE ORDERED dinner sent up to his suite, dismissed the servants, arranged for one of the building waiters to serve the dinner and then disappear. Sat down to wait.

When at last she came, he was even more impressed than he had been at first sight of her. She was using a perfume a little stronger than strict good taste permits; but in her he didn't mind it. It created around her a delicious, exotic pagan atmosphere, as the sweetish odor mingled with the vitalizing girlish aroma of her youthfulness and ripeness as a young female.

She was dressed as simply tonight as she had been the night before. Paul took her wrap. They had a cocktail, chatted a while in a neutral manner, then went in to dinner. Over dinner she said:

"It was certainly great of you to take an interest in me; but I'm afraid that I won't be of any use to you."

"I think you may put your fears at rest on that score at once," Paul smiled.

"I'm afraid not," she sighed. "You see, we've always been poor. I never had any music lessons, or dancing lessons, or anything like that. If I can neither sing or dance—and I certainly couldn't speak lines—what earthly use would I be to a theatrical producer?"

"Plenty," Paul smiled back boldly.

"But it takes talent to be an actress," she observed, "and I am afraid I may not have any talent at all; I haven't had the slightest experience. I sell hosiery in a department store."

"My dear," he told her; "you've been reading cheap novels. You've got all it takes to become an actress nowadays. It isn't what you *do* on the stage any more; it's what you are.—And I think you've got it all for my purposes.

"You see, I hire a few competent actors and actresses to do comedy turns and some dancing; but the backbone of my shows are the chorus and the various tableaux. That's what people pay high prices at my box office to see. And since the dawn of time people have paid high prices to see such things; and until time has ticked off its last tick, people will still pay high prices to see such things."

"I think I get you," she giggled; "but, gee, I've seen some shows like that, and I'd be embarrassed to death."

"—Needlessly," he told her; "why should you be embarrassed at revealing your perfections? That's what nature gave them to you for."

"Maybe—" she smiled. Paul had seen to it that her wine glass was repeatedly filled. Probably, he thought, she had never before tasted wine of that quality. And it was wine with a body to it that went down easily but raised hell when it got down.

When they had finished dinner, the building functionary Paul had borrowed cleared off the table and left only a fresh bottle of wine and their glasses and an ash tray.

"Of course," Paul went on, "I'd have to assure myself of your, er—perfections, absolutely, before going into the matter of a contract. However, there's this to consider:

"I think you are one of the most exceptional beauties I have ever found. If you attract unusual attention in one of my shows, with the consequent publicity, you may have a chance to get into the movies. For all you know, a year, or two years from today, you may be a great star, known from coast to coast, your picture in all the magazines and newspapers, frequently. Don't you think, in view of all that, you might be able to overcome a little of your embarrassment?"

"I shouldn't wonder," she said.

"Let's go into the other room," Paul suggested. As he walked behind her into the next room Paul observed with shudders of ecstasy the lithe sway of her hips, the revealing way in which her inexpensive gown clung for a moment to her sleek, slender straight young limbs, then teasingly fell into amorphous shape snatching away sight of her dainties of curvature.

THEY sat down upon a divan in the large front living room of Paul's luxurious suite.

Thomasine was flushed and excited. She sat down upon the divan with averted eyes.

"You don't need to be at all embarrassed," he began.—You see, a theatrical producer gets to be just like an artist or a doctor. Such matters are part of his business, he thinks nothing of them."

"You mean that you want to see—" she faltered, and glanced wildly into his eyes, then away.

"If you don't mind—"

"You should be proud," said Paul.

"Oh—! But!—" she began. Then went on after a minute; "I hope you won't get impatient with me; only, well, although I'm certainly no silly prudish kid, I never before let any man see—that is, this sort of thing is all new to me, and I feel, feel—"

"Don't be afraid," Paul coaxed gently. Her fingers were toying with her shoulder straps. They slipped easily over her smoothly rounded pink white warm young shoulders. Thomasine said: "Oh! Oh! Please—!" and covered her face with her hands. But she did not move to interfere with Paul's inspection. Paul feared to frighten her. He forced composure and said crisply, like a doctor:

"Very satisfactory indeed; you should be proud." At this she took her hands down from her face and looked bashfully up at him. Reassured, apparently, she put her hands in her lap and was quite docile.

"You have beautiful shoulders too," he congratulated. "It is very important, however, that there be no blemishes upon the upper part of the body. The torso should rise slim and smooth as a white ivory column from the waist; I wonder do you fit these requirements?"

"Oh please," she got out, "some other time perhaps; only—!"

"There is," Paul assured her firmly, "no time like the present." Before she could take alarm and flee, he had induced her to remain. She took a deep breath, as though someone had thrown a glass of cold water on her chest.—Trembled. Avoided his eyes.

"Superb!" Paul congratulated. And he was very much in earnest. Not a blemish the size of a pin head. Perfect satin white warm flesh, quivering just slightly under her tremors. He could feel the blood pounding at his temples; strove to keep his hands from obviously trembling.

"You're splendid," he encouraged, "lots of girls, never having had any experience before,

She glanced wildly into his eyes.

would have acted dreadfully silly under such inspection. Really, there's nothing to it. Artists, you know, require their models to pose in the nude in all sorts of positions.

"In fact, one of my coming tableaux is to be somewhat on that order. There will be several models, posing for a mural, while an artist on the stage before them makes sketches on a large canvas. Of course there will be gauze curtains between the models and the audience, but these gauze curtains will be lifted one by one, according to how far we may dare to go this season. Naturally, behind the gauze curtains, the subjects will be wholly undraped. Therefore, you see, it is necessary that I absolutely assure myself about everything. If you don't mind standing up now for a moment."

"I couldn't; really I couldn't," she begged. "Not that—please."

"You don't by any chance prefer selling hosiery to the life of a successful actress, do you?" he asked pleasantly.

"Oh, no indeed," she agreed; "but, you see, I—"

Gently he urged her to her feet, where she stood ashamed and looking the other way, hanging on tightly to her gown. A fever of impatience was upon him; but he forced himself to go slowly.

"If you'd rather call the inspection off for tonight," he suggested, "and return some other time when you would be better prepared for such an examination—"

"No," she said; "I could just as well do it tonight as at any other time; I suppose I'm dreadfully silly to act this way. I hope you won't lose patience altogether and, and—"

"There!" Paul said. "Now it's done." For she had finally pushed everything aside, so that she stood a marvelously beautiful slim white column of girlhood just budding into womanhood before him. With a little shamed cry she threw her arm up over her face protectingly. But the worst of it was over now. With another ten minutes' coaxing, Paul succeeded in getting her to assume various poses which he suggested.

Never had he seen such exquisite feminine contours; such whiteness and softness and warmth. Never had he exerted so much control as now he must exert to behave as he watched the white nymph, clad now in black stockings and high heeled shoes, assume artistic poses at his command.

At last he could contain himself no longer. At first she struggled like a frightened deer; but when he fastened his lips expertly and warmly upon hers, she relaxed in his arms with a little half frightened, half happy sigh.

It was later, when she had resumed her gown, that some subtle change came over her. Paul got the wine and filled their glasses. She eyed him almost maliciously over the top of her glass as she sipped. She had tucked the contract which he had signed into the bosom of her dress.

"You'll have dinner with me again tomorrow night," he said, anxiously. She laughed lightly.

"No"

"But I love you—"

"Yes," she laughed; "but we'll have no more dates—because, you see—well—there just won't be any more, that's all."

"You're suffering [*Continued on page 56*]

Clap Hands, There Goes Charlie!

WORD comes from Ziegfeld offices that there will be no chorus men in the new Follies! Well, well—another ancient and honorable custom has gone by, and *"whoops dearie"* will be just a forgotten phrase around Mr. Ziegfeld's showshop on Sixth Avenue!

Mr. Heywood, the famous gent who tells you all about the Stage, tells me that there aren't to be any chorus girls in several new shows—that makes Broadway a candidate for oblivion! What, no chorus girls — or men! We don't give a damn about the men, but bring back those gals!

Dear Old Belle Again

OUR old friend Belle Livingstone, who has operated the swankiest places for thirsty New Yorkers (and who has been in jail for doing it) has a Grand Inspiration this time—she's going to pack up her sin den and move it to Reno. Suppose Belle will throw in a divorce with every case of D. T.s!

There are to be no chorus girls in several new shows.

$20,000 For Inez

IF YOU have been following your tabloids, you know that the late Arnold Rothstein left his estate in a rather mixed up condition. However they say that Inez Norton, the pretty lady who stuck by him through thick and thin, (she got her training for this in the FOLLIES) has been awarded $20,000 for her trouble.

The moral of this yarn is: IT PAYS TO BE KIND, GIRLS!

Tcht, Tcht

GOOD old Broadway was the Apple Sellers Paradise a year ago, but now there are only three apple men left on the Main Stem. It looks as if the Actors and Night Clubbers were so short of cash they can't even keep their girls in apples! It's a good thing Adam and Eve aren't living now!

Nice For Aviators!

FOX is building a roof garden on top of the Roxy Theatre, where his little hot and tired chorus girls can go and relax—take off their bloomers and stretch in the sun.

What a break for the aviators! This also should boost the renting of offices in the Chrysler and Empire State Buildings—we'll be right there opening day, in our merry old balloon!

The Pay Off!

A LOT of funny things have been written about the failure of the Bank of the U. S. (funny, if you didn't happen to lose any jack) but the one that takes the cake is the true tale about the dumb dora who had been presented with ten thousand berries by her sugar daddy. She deposited the gold in the bank of the U. S. . . . but one day someone tipped her off that the bank was going busto. [*Continued on page* 63]

Love—to Order

[*Continued from page* 25]

Tom put an arm about her. He glared at Carter. Carter glared back.

"Get out!" commanded Tom.

Carter managed a convincing sneer.

"I've got as much right here as any man!" he retorted. "I love Midgie. I've loved her for months. She's got to be mine. I'm crazy about her!"

"You're drunk!" snapped Tom.

"I'm not drunk!" roared Carter so savagely that even Midgie could not repress a slight shudder. "Look here, Midgie. For the last time, will you come with me, or will you not?"

His face worked, his eyes dilated. Even Tom took a step backward at the apparent torment of a man in love that he was undergoing.

"No," said Midgie faintly. "I told you I don't care for you. Tom Wilson here is the man I love. Now please be reasonable and go."

"I see!" cried Carter as if possessed. His laugh would have made the blood of a Hottentot run cold. "Well, don't say I didn't warn you."

With a swift movement he extracted the revolver and lifted it to his forehead.

For a moment there was a pause in which you could have heard your heart beat. Then, just as his finger tightened on the trigger, there was a scream from Midgie and an oath from Tom. Tom rushed over and tried to wrest the gun from Carter's hand.

He succeeded, though Carter put up a pretty good imitation of a fight. In fact, quite a bit of furniture was wrecked before Tom stood up, put the gun in his pocket, and lifted Carter to his feet.

And then, to the astonishment of both Carter and Midgie, Tom put out his hand to his supposed rival in love.

"Don't take on so, old man," he said, and in his voice was real sympathy. "I understand how you feel. Midgie is a great kid. I can understand why you love her the way you do. In fact, I can see that your love for her is a lot bigger than mine. Old man, I can't stand in the way of a love like yours. I came here tonight to tell Midgie I was ready to divorce my wife and marry her. But I can never give her the love you can give her. I resign her to you. Goodbye and good luck to both of you."

And he grasped Midgie, pushed her into Carter's arms, and swiftly left the boudoir.

The two plotters stared at each other.

"He's gone! Tom is gone!" cried Midgie. "He wasn't fooled a bit, the big fish. Oh, what an idea this was to get him jealous and make sure he would want me. Oh, what'll I do now. What'll I do?"

Carter looked at her. For the first time that night his eyes kindled.

"Midgie," he said, and his voice trembled with real emotion this time, "I'll be frank with you. When I started loving you to order tonight, I didn't care about you. It was work. But, Midgie, my whole attitude has changed. I'm in love with my job. Imitating love has brought on an attack of the real thing. Midgie, I love you—I—"

She smiled. "Well, if you make love the way you did when you're only doing it to order, I wonder how you'll act when you really mean it?"

And to find out she did a little dance for him then and there. Excited by her violent motion the chemise yielded gracefully to the force of gravity. The step-ins followed. Soon she was gyrating before him dressed only in nature's best.

And as Carter caught her in his arms and proceeded to act out his applause, he realized that he had won his sweetheart after all. What did it matter that she wasn't the one he had set out to win? He didn't mind.

Neither did Midgie!

Honors Even

[*Continued from page* 54]

superficial remorse," he told her; "but, in twenty-four hours you'll get over it."

"On the contrary," she said, "I am suffering no remorse or regrets at all. I am quite happy. You see, I didn't expect to like you at all . . but when finally I met you I *did* like you quite a lot. If I had put something over on you and not been charming with you, I would have suffered from some small degree of remorse afterward; but, as it is . . . well, I shall never feel that I treated you too shamefully. I was, to some extent, nice to you; not, of course, because of any latent altruism on my part; I enjoyed the evening *tremendously*."

"What do you mean?" he asked suspiciously, wondering what on earth she could be hinting at.

She rose and moved toward the door. Opened it. Stood for a moment in it smiling enigmatically.

"You'll find out soon enough," she smiled, and, closing the door, was gone, leaving Paul standing in the middle of the floor suddenly very thoughtful. What could it mean? Blackmail? A frame-up of some kind? He strode the floor in perplexed anxiety. But all that night nothing happened.

And then, at dinner next day, he saw the evening papers.

He stared, in amazement, at his picture on the front page, beside the picture of Thomasine. Eagerly he went into the lead:

"Society Girl Tricks Producer."

"Miss Thomasine Corminster, Gets Contract From Broadway's Pulchritude Picker."

Followed a long account of how, several days before, Paul Mordaunt had, in a press interview, claimed that the working girls of New York, the daughters of the proletariat and the bourgeoise had it all over the society girls when it came to beauty. He remembered the fool interview, recalled that he had thought up the thing as a publicity stunt. He had forgotten all about it; but now he saw it all.

Thomasine had easily enough found out places he frequented; had appeared before him, flirted with him, made a fool out of him. Yes, made the very devil of a fool out of him, because, on an inside page, was a photograph of the contract he had given her, after he had said in his newspaper interview that there wasn't a society girl in New York pretty enough to get a part in a Mordaunt review. He would be laughed at endlessly.

Paul got up and strode the floor. There was only one way to get even. And how much he would enjoy that way. Perhaps she had fooled him; but would *she* be able to forget last night? To marry Thomasine . . . would be to gain Heaven. It would be hard; but it was worth trying. He grinned as he fished out of his pocket the card that bore her telephone number and stepped to the 'phone.

HOLDING UP THE STAGE

By HOLWORTH HEYWOOD

A Pip, And How!

BY FAR the niftiest revue in seven years is THE BANDWAGON, and if you can get a ticket by begging, borrowing or stealing, my advice to you is to hop right to it, no matter the price! (Of course, if you happen to be a charming young lady with lots of *it, these* and *thosem,* your heavy boy friend will probably take you, but for the rest of us poor fish it's going to be harder!)

The Agile Astaires

FRED and Adele Astaire are the stars, and co-starred with them are Frank Morgan (late star of TOPAZE), Helen Broderick, and the gorgeous, willowy dancer, Tilly Losch. Speaking of Tilly, she is the one, we've decided, that we'd pick for that desert island that everyone dreams of—you must see Tilly shake her stuff!

But we must pass most of the boquets to the Astaires, for it is their show, and they really make it the smash hit that it is. Just to show you how hard we work for you, dear readers, we journeyed clear (but not clean) over to Philadelphia to witness the opening of THE BANDWAGON, so we could rush to press with this account, before the show opened in New York.

Of course, by the time you read these lines, the show will be a Grrr—and and Glll—orious success in Gotham, but don't say we didn't tell you!

Some Hot Shots

TWO of the high points of THE BANDWAGON are as follows, now hold your breath Eustice! A man is murdered, and instead of taking the fingerprints, the detective insists that every suspected person sit in a softly cushioned chair for an imprint of their sitting apparatus. It seems, according to the detective that "there are no two alike."

And, by golly, they can't find the murderer—until, zippo, some one discovers that the butler is wearing a false bottom! Ha-ha-ha, and a dozen or so tee hees!

Then There's The One About—

WELL, it seems a lady in another scene is thinking of building a couple of new bathrooms in her house, so she arrives at a bathroom showroom to look around. It also seems they demonstrate every item they sell—so you can guess the plight of the poor lady! Tcht, tcht! Aren't these revues the naughtiest things!

Fred Has A New Act

FRED WARING, whose band recently appeared in THE NEW YORKERS, is playing vaudeville and has a fast and furious new act. It opens with "THE JAY HOP" as hot a sizzler as you ever heard, and goes from one sprightly tune to another, until the high point is reached when Evalyn Nair dashes out and does a Collegiate Hooch dance to the tune of "Sweet and Hot."

This Nair baby sends the boys into fits and hysterics, and when it comes to juggling the anatomy, she knows how to do it to the Queen's (or rather, KING'S taste! [*Continued on page* 62]

She's the one we'd pick for that desert island.

WHATS NEW IN HOLLYWOOD

Gloria's New One

GLORIA SWANSON (who, incidentally, has the smallest feet of any motion picture star—she wears shoes size two!) is going to brave the mike once again in a picture called *Obey That Impulse.* The story will be by that champion triumvirate, DeSylva, Brown and Henderson.

We're all hot and bothered waiting to see Gloria—for, let them come and go, Gloria packs a mean wallop, and possesses more than her share of the well known box office Sex Appeal!

A Lot Of Jack!

WELL, well! Rumor has it that in spite of John Gilbert's so-so attempts at talking pictures, the film company has again signed him to make four new pictures, and at a salary (hold your breath my dears) of one million bucks, smackers, iron men, or whatever is your pet name for dough. Who said Jack was an object of pity? And speaking of big money (it's a lot of fun to talk about it) what do you think of little Ann Harding?

She has jumped from $1,500 a week up to the grand sum of $6,000 a week! No wonder they charge a dollar to get in the de luxe cinema palaces! . . . . personally, little Eugenia would rather have them chop a few thousand dollars a week from the stars' salaries, and give us poor movie fans a better break at the box office. Let's start a movement, or something!

At Last We Know!

ALMOST everybody in the good old U. S. A. has been taking a guess at how to pronounce "Marlene", the front tag of the Devilish Dietrich. Well, Miss Dietrich herself says that the correct way to say her first name is "MAR-LEE-NA," . . . so there, now, you know all about it!

And did you see her in *Dishonored?* Li'l Eugenia was rather disappointed, but perhaps our hopes were set too high after her sexy performance in *Morocco,* and *The Last Laugh.*

Speaking of sex, which we seem to be doing quite often, there was more condensed sex in *The Last Laugh* than has appeared in any film of the last two years . . . of course, if you were unfortunate enough to live in some of the states which cut out the racy parts, well that's just too bad. We saw the original version, and nearly swallowed our gum!

Come On, Joan

JOAN CRAWFORD, who has a yen to follow in the footsteps of the Great, Glorious Greta, had better hunt around for a better story than *Dance Fools Dance* if she wants to bowl over this little department. We sat through the above flicker expecting something to happen every minute—but it never did.

We'd like to vote this chinema the poorest in many a moon! Look at your stories, Joan, or you'll have to starting stripping down to your cuticle and display lots of teddies and filmy underwear, like you did in the good old days that made you famous.

Can You Beat It?

A LOT has been said about the clamor for stardom. Folks would have you believe that every picture player is just all itchy and nuts to see their name in electric lights, over the name of the picture—a star, in other words.

But such isn't always the case, for only last month Marie Dressler and Adolphe Menjou absolutely refused to be starred! Gurgle over that one!

And to add to the list of pictureites who just work for Work's Sake, Frederic March, Wallace Beery and Dorothy Lee. Yes sir, they also refused to be starred. WHAT is the industry coming to!?

Are You A Golfer?

GOLF FANS have been going plain cuckoo over the golf shorts that Bobby Jones has been making. They have been drawing more customers than the feature flickers themselves . . . honest injun! But if you are one of the fans who have rushed to the box office with your pennies, perhaps you've wondered why Bobby looked so funny.

He refused to use any make-up for the series, proving something or other . . . probably that he didn't want the men to think he is a pansy!

Pet Superstitions

ADDING to our former list of little superstitions of the squawkie stars, here comes the news that Janet Gaynor always wears the pair of shoes she wore in *Seventh Heaven* in every picture she makes . . . just for luck, y'know.

GLORIA SWANSON

And Edmund Lowe, they'll have you believe, always makes up in his college freshman cap . . . and Dick Arlen hugs tightly to the aviator's helmet he wore in *Wings,* the picture that made him a big shot.

Last Minute News

CHARMING Victor McLaglen has a son 10 years old . . . rather late to announce it Vic! . . . Wallace Beery is the only film actor who holds a transport airplane license . . . you can transport us any time you say, Wally! . . . Charles Butterworth never laughs on the screen—or off! . . . Jackie Coogan is demanding over a thousand dollars a day to appear in more pictures . . . oooooch! . . . Dick Arlen and Jobyna are nerts about puzzles, and give puzzle parties. We went to a puzzle party once, the puzzle was who stole the gin!

Be Sure And See (All AAAA Films)

Transatlantic, with Joan Bennett and Victor McLaglen.

Wicked, with Elissa Landi, Spencer Tracy and V. McLaglen.

Skyline, bringing back dear Thomas Meighan, and Maureen O'Sullivan . . . and Myrna Loy. We can't imagine what Myrna is doing with so many good looking Irishmen!

Toodle ooo, till next month,

—EUGENIA VALLE.

Madcap Magda

[*Continued from page* 18]

"'Nother drink," she demanded. He got her another drink; got himself one. This was the third, large hooker of straight whiskey she had had; apparently she had never heard of a chaser. She was plainly affected now. Ackroyd began to get worried again. From drowning in a huge chaser, she had about turned to drowning in liquor. Her head began to nod dizzily, as he rubbed. He stopped in anxiety.

"Hey, keep it up," she demanded; "it's swell. Kiss me, burglar."

He hurried for the cupboard, for a steadying drink; from force of habit brought two. She grabbed one and threw it down.

"Mus' be drunk, burglar," she told him a minute later. "If drunk can dance swell, wanna see? Turn on the phonograph. Put on somethin' plenty hot. Ackroyd reached for a record. Everything Hayden had in the cabinet was hot so it didn't make any difference. Soon he was swaying dizzily around the floor with her. They had some more drinks; and then danced some more.

When this finally ended, Ackroyd could not have told. He opened his eyes, it seemed to him a few minutes later, to find that the reason he had opened them was that the sun was impolitely staring him in the face. He looked around, puzzled, hardly knowing where he was. Not far away he saw Magda lying on the floor, breathing regularly the deep breaths of a heavy sleeper.

Gradually the events of the day before came back to him. He got heavily to his feet. The thought of tasting a drop of liquor was like the thought of drinking carbolic acid; but he knew that hard as the first drink might be to get down, it would change everything, once down, and be far better than drinking the ocean of ice water he longed for. He took a stiff hooker from the cupboard. Went out to the car. Got some eggs and bacon and coffee and bread. . . . Came back and started breakfast.

It was after the aroma of frying eggs and bacon had floated through the house, through the kitchen door left open, that she came walking out into the kitchen.

"Jez! Burglar, you can cook, too!" she observed with satisfaction. "Everybody should have a little burglar like you in their home. A burglar who can wrestle and kiss and cook; why, that's even better than Companionate Marriage at its best. Any whiskey left in that keg?"

"Now listen," Ackroyd began, "please—"

"I'm dying," she told him; "even a condemned person is entitled to a last breakfast; and I'm going to eat some of that breakfast if it's the last thing I do; and I can't eat unless I have something to brace me up. Would you have me die?"

"No indeed," Ackroyd told her, and he was surprised at the fervor in his tone. She seemed surprised, too, and gave him a quick look.

"You kind of like me, don't you, burglar," she observed.

"Indeed I do," he told her.

"Well, kiss me," she suggested.

"Now look here," Ackroyd said, "this thing has got to end somewhere. I'm no burglar. My name's Ackroyd, and I'm a stock broker. Mr. Hayden, who owns this house, gave me the keys and told me that I could come out here for some peace and quiet; I've had a terrible time on a falling market on the Exchange, for months.

"I think you're the prettiest thing I ever saw, and I'm crazy about you; but I can't go on rescuing you from drowning, and dressing you, and rubbing your hair, and kissing you indefinitely, without serious damage to your reputation. I'd suggest that you sober up, think things over, try to remember what your name is, and where you fit; and let me take you there, after you've thought up an appropriate excuse for staying out all night.

"I'd like nothing better than to have you stay with me here for a week; but I am not forgetful of the fix that might put you in. Your folks probably have the police out looking for you now; your mother is unquestionably enjoying a priceless fit of hysterics, and your father is probably talking about all kinds of things that he would like to inflict upon John Doe. Do I make myself clear?"

"Perfectly," she told him. "What did you say?"

"I said sit down and have some breakfast," he told her; "it's all ready."

They sat down in the kitchen, at the white kitchen table, with the sun streaming in, and the birds singing outside.

"Just like being married," she said, moodily.

"Precisely," he smiled. " . . . Only, I don't believe, much, in marriage; it's so stuffy, with the man jealously watching the woman, and the woman jealously watching the man—and both of them cramping each other's styles frightfully."

She put down the piece of toast she had been about to munch and stared at him in surprise.

"Say, burglar, stockbroker, I mean, I like you; that's the way I feel about marriage too. Everybody wants me to get married; but I wouldn't for the world. I like to make whoopee, to live, to be free, all that . . . "

"Me too," Ackroyd agreed; "although, after all, marriage might be made a beautiful thing, between two souls who weren't conventional. They could be pals, instead of stuffy old married folks. Enjoying each other's company when they wanted to, and enjoying the company of other members of the opposite sex when they wanted to; of course, that kind of marriage might not work—but everybody *knows* the other kind doesn't."

"Burglar—stockbroker, I mean," she returned, "you're a regular fellow. What do you say we get married like that? If it don't work there's nothing lost—and maybe, then, they'd let me alone to do as I pleased. Yes, I think I'll marry you—what did you say your name was?"

"Ackroyd," he told her; "the name is *Ackroyd*. If you're going to marry me, will you please try to remember it?"

"I'll try," she promised. It was then that they heard the front door being opened; heard steps along the hall; the steps hesitated, then came on into the kitchen. Ackroyd jumped up as Hayden entered the room.

"Hello old man," Hayden greeted. "Hello Sis."

"Sis!" Ackroyd almost shouted. "Sis! Sis!"

"Want you to meet one of the swellest burglars—no, I mean stockbrokers I ever saw," she said to her brother; "his name is, is—what did you say your name was?"

But Ackroyd was wild. He dragged Hayden into the other room.

"What the devil does this mean?" he demanded of Hayden angrily. Hayden looked up at him sheepishly.

"Gee! Old Man!" he said, "forgive me, maybe I did wrong; but, you see . . . although Sis is nearly twenty, she never finished college. She got fired too many times. She got fired again the other day, for getting lit at chapel, and the folks were so sore she didn't dare go home. I sent her off up here. She's the problem of the family; the swellest little girl in the world, but no good in last century's harness. The folks are conventional, and like most kids of conventional families, there's no holding her.

"I knew she was here when I sent you out. I took a long chance. I knew you were unconventional, and had nothing but contempt, like her, for last generation Behavior Patterns; it was a desperate experiment, but something had to be done. If anybody could hold her, a man like you could; and even if you couldn't, Sis is a great girl, and even a marriage with her that ended in divorce wouldn't be so bad. . . Then she'd be a Mrs. and you wouldn't have missed anything appertaining to life. Will you ever forgive me?"

"Forgive you," Ackroyd grinned; "I wouldn't have missed her for worlds; she's just what I need as a reaction from too much stockbrokering. An ordinary woman as wife would bore me to tears—I want wild excitement to steady the nerves when I get away from the stock exchange; I know this sylvan retreat notion wouldn't work at all . . . I'd have been back in town this morning if it hadn't been for her. She's wonderful.

"If there is any way on earth to get her to remember my name, and stop calling me a burglar, I'll marry her today and—we'll spend one night's honeymoon back here tonight, if you don't mind."

"By jez! It worked!" Hayden said, and he breathed a heartfelt sigh up deep from the pit of his stomach.

On With The Trance

[*Continued from page* 36]

In amazement, Dave watched her perfectly normal movements.

"Say," he demanded wonderingly, "how did that alarm get set for twelve o'clock?"

"I set it, myself," said Madge, flushing slightly. "I set it when you went looking for your book of instructions."

Dave tried to absorb this statement, but failed.

"You couldn't have," he said. "You were in a trance. Your mind was a blank. That is—" he faltered uncertainly, "—it was, unless—unless— Madge!" he cried in sudden alarm. "Do you mean to tell me that all this time you weren't—weren't hypnotized?"

"Well—" began Madge, dubiously.

"You weren't!" groaned Dave, divining the truth. "What'll I do? The act is ruined, a failure! And I thought you were in a trance all the time! And I'm just another ham actor, I guess."

"Well," admitted Madge, roguishly, "I wasn't exactly in a trance. But at the same time, Dave, your act wasn't altogether a flop. No, it went over big! Come here," she commanded, stretching out her arms. "Kiss me, Dave. If you want, you've just got time to make that Buffalo train with the Dancing Dahls. You can be our business manager, and hypnotize theatre owners into giving us the best spot on the bills!"

Don't Fail to Read PETTING PATSY, *by Sally Delmar, in the next SNAPPY; It's One of the Livest Little Stories of the Year.*

Hiking to Love

[*Continued from page* 12]

over your natural fright at such a big place—perhaps I shall take you back to Chicago with me. At any rate, I'm going to work everything out for you. Understand that. I'll take a supreme pleasure in doing so."

At the hotel he went up to the room with her. Saw her safely in and then turned toward the door. But as he started to leave, a large tear stole down her cheek. In a moment he was back and at her side. . . . Had her soft form in his arms, holding her close. She trembled a little, as from fright; but pressed herself to him, wanting to be held close.

"Couldn't you just stay here," she begged, "and be good?"

"All right," he told her. "I'll stay."

While she undressed, he looked again out of the window; but this time the night had turned the window into a mirror, and he could see her splendid body in all its smooth whiteness, as she wriggled out of things and into one of the dainty pairs of pajamas he had bought her.

With veins distended from the beating of his heart, Alan turned out the light and, himself, prepared for what sleep he might be able to get on the divan in the room.

He had hardly composed himself to attempt sleep before one of those sudden summer storms that follow hot days in New York broke with fury. At the first crash of thunder she cried out in fright. Alan rose and went across to her. Took her soft body, its heat so little confined by the thin stuff of her pajamas, into his arms.

He felt her jump with nervous fear every time the lightning flashed, to be followed by a deafening crash of thunder. Something about the wildness of the storm whipped his nervous system to frenzies. He found himself kissing her small mouth, crushing it with his lips. Shyly at first, but more and more bold, she returned his kisses, responded to his caresses.

Forgotten was the fury of the storm, which still flashed outside. The storm worked slowly up to a peak; then, in wild incontinence, broke and came down upon the city like the end of the world. Then gradually, during the hour that followed, it quieted down, renewed a little, now and then, but never quite attained a high peak again.

When Alan awoke in the morning, he was alone in the room. Even all of the dainty, intimate things were gone. She had packed them in the suitcase and overnight bag he had bought her and fled.

Alan sprang up . . . . He did not give a thought to the money he was out; and he assured himself by looking in his wallet that she had indeed taken a hundred or two that was in that, too. The money was nothing. It was her that he disliked losing . . . For her perfumed, almost childish loveliness was still upon him like an obsession. He could feel the warmth of her perfect curvature against him . . . Could sense the fragrance of her young womanhood as though unseen flowers were about.

On the dresser there was a note, written in a childish scrawl.

"I never disliked my racket so much as I did this morning when I awoke to run away. You see, I pull that right along . . . dressing up like a boy and tramping the roads into New York to be picked up. Usually those who pick me up are quite nasty, and I take supreme pleasure in gyping them. But you . . . you were so different. I really fell in love with you. So much so, in fact, that for a time I considered making you love me enough to marry me. But that, I thought, was worse than stealing out on you; so I did the latter. At any rate, you have one satisfaction . . . you are the first one I ever gyped that made me ashamed to do it. When I get enough money I'm going to Europe. I want to see all the world. And I'll *never* forget *you*; you were so different. Goodbye,

Grace."

Alan's hand trembled as he held the note. Just then the 'phone rang. It was the house detective.

"Just caught a moll sneaking out," that worthy informed Alan; "I think she came from your room. Want me to hold her? Or is it jake to let her go?—it's all up to you."

"Hold her," Alan directed gleefully. "I'll be right down."

He dressed swiftly, and as he dressed he thought of her exquisite beauty, and of the dainty little love nests with which the Gold Coast, in Chicago, abounded.

Holding Up The Stage

[*Continued from page* 57]

Fritz Kreisler A Songwriter!

FRITZ KREISLER, the well-known fiddler, is going to write the music for a new musical comedy to be produced this fall by Vincent Youmans.

Vincent, you know, is no mean songwriter himself, having turned out TEA FOR TWO, HALLELULAH, I WANT TO BE HAPPY, and no end of other feet ticklers. Turn about is fair play, so Vincent should learn to play the violin if Kreisler is going to steal his thunder!

Melo, A Record

THE play MELO that has to do with a naughty wife who falls in love with a musician and merely kills her hubby so she can carry on the affair without interference, was brought over by the Shuberts, and they paid the record sum of six thousand berries advance royalty to the author.

The show has been a sensation in New York, but the sad news is that Edna Best (who plays the part of the wife) has become lonesome for her real husband in London, and is going to leave the show cold and dash over to her turtle dove.

Chorusless Musical Comedies!

AS IF times weren't tough enough, the Shuberts are going to produce a series of musical comedies minus the pretty pretties who dash out ever so often without much on their cute little figgers!

Well, it may be oke, but we'll bet our last year's gin bottles that the first ten rows will be vacant! Imagine a bald headed row at a leg show without any legs!

Speaking Of Heat—

IF YOU want a load of real red hot stuff in the form of melodrama, get a peek (if the police don't close it) at the new show called "HONOR CODE" produced by Jack Linder . . . the lad who projected Mae West in some of her naughty drammers.

The plot of HONOR CODE has to do with grizzly men who force their love on young pretty girls, then get shot, and hell is raised in general. Plenty of heat . . . but Holworth is having plenty right now. See you later!

Looking Over Broadway

[*Continued from page* 55]

So the little blonde rushed to the bank, drew out her money . . . then got in a taxi to look for *another* bank. She saw a pretty bank and dashed in, depositing her money. The next day she discovered that she had put her coin in *another* branch of the Bank of the U. S. And they hang photographs!

Daddy Again

ONE of Broadway's familiar figures is getting it in the neck again. Dear old Daddy Browning is being sued by the little gal who thought he was going to adopt her. It seems she got stubborn or something and he playfully spanked her.

She says she's still sore, and that the spank is worth plenty of sugar. Good old Sugar Daddy Browning! By the way, this gal we're speaking of isn't Peaches—no, no. It's the Spas chicadee, present name Mary Spas Tvrdy!

Pete Arno Draws A New One

PETER ARNO, who shocks the old ladies in Iowa with his hilarious drawings in the *New Yorker,* has gone to Reno to get rid of his writing wifey, Lois Long, and has drawn a new pip in the person of Florence Rice, also being divorced.

Harlem Hot Spots

THOSE red-nosed play boys who get a big kick out of undraped ebony gals are flocking to the new hidden show places of the negro section . . . where you have to have a card to get in and a blank check to get out!

We've heard that the dances they put on up there are just nobody's business, and when it comes to wriggles, the blacker they come the faster they wiggle.

The old standbys, of course, are CONNIE'S INN and THE COTTON CLUB, but if you want the real stuff, just whisper in any colored taxi driver's ear . . . and he'll show you the sights.

And with that little tip, we'll sign off till next time!

—TIMES SQUARE.

Never Say Dice!

[*Continued from page* 42]

tossed a bathrobe to her. "It's finished—you may look at it now!" he said, and there was something of awe, of worship, in his voice.

She approached the canvas—and drew a sharp breath. "Oh, Jimmie —it—it's beautiful!" she whispered. Then she blushed. "Does that sound egotistical?"

He whirled toward her. "Egotistical? You sweet little straw-haired angel from hell, you've a right to be egotistical! You're beautiful—you're divine! The picture's not half as wonderful as you are—"

She backed away from him. "Mustn't touch, Jimmie. Remember our bargain!"

His face clouded. Then he turned to the newly-finished portrait. "Well," he grunted, "at least I've got this—and if I want to worship it, nobody's going to stop me!"

She touched his arm. "Jimmie—I don't want you to have that picture," she said. "I—I just couldn't bear the idea of its being here, and your looking at it all the time. And I can't even stand the thought of your exhibiting it in public—"

He laughed harshly. "Never fear. I'll never exhibit it. It's *you*—and a man doesn't put the woman he loves on exhibition in the nude!"

"Jimmie, I want that picture!" she said again.

He stared at her. "Are you batty, April? I wouldn't sell that thing for all the money in the world!"

"But—I want it!" she affirmed again.

He smiled sourly. "Try and get it, Miss Teaser!"

She opened her blue eyes, wide and shining. "Listen, Jimmie—you said I was afraid to gamble with you, three weeks ago . . . remember? You accused me of being afraid to—to gamble with stakes other than money. I—I proved you wrong, didn't I? I played the game, didn't I? And when I lost, I—posed for you the way you wanted?"

He nodded, puzzled. "Yes. What are you getting at? I took back all I ever said about you being a welcher."

She was close to him. Her voice was hard, metallic. "Well, Jimmie —let's see if you're as good a gambler as I am! I want that picture—and you don't want to sell it. I probably couldn't afford it if you would part with it for money. Well, let's see what kind of sport you are. I'll gamble you for that picture!"

He stared at her in amazement. "Why, you little simpleton!" he answered harshly. "What kind of one-sided gamble would that be? You admit you haven't enough money to risk against the picture. What would I get *if you lost?*"

She blushed and her voice sank very low. "I—I'll call off our bargain about—the—the kisses, if I lose, Jimmie," she said. Then her chin went up. "But if I win, I want that picture!"

He hesitated.

"Welching?" she said swiftly.

He flushed. "No!" he shouted. "Damn you, April, I'll take you on!"

Like a flash she dashed to her dressing-room. She returned with a coin. "Heads, I get the picture. Tails, you keep it and—I release you from your promises!" she breathed . . . and flipped the coin.

It fell to the floor, spun—and came to rest, tails up!

She picked it up. "You win, Jimmie!" she said simply.

He crushed her into his arms. His mouth found her mouth, forced it open . . . smothered it ravenously . . .

Then he picked her up and carried her out of the studio, into his own quarters . . .

An hour later, Jimmie was saying: "We'll go right out and get married, darling. Oh, my dear—my dear!" he whispered into her ear. His lips brushed her white neck.

An hour after that, they were back in the studio. April Wallice was April Wallice no longer. She was Mrs. Jimmie MacAleer.

Jimmie confronted her. "April —my wife—angel-devil!" he said. She came close to him. He held her very tightly. "I—I have a confession to make," he whispered.

She looked into his eyes. "What is it, sweet?"

He blushed. "You know—when we shot dice—to see if you'd pose clothed or in the nude?"

She nodded.

"Well—remember I picked up the dice and put them behind me for luck?"

She nodded again.

He blushed more deeply. "I—I switched dice!" he confessed. "I substituted loaded dice, so I'd win—so you'd have to pose in the nude!"

Her mouth formed a surprised O. He hung his head. "Do you hate me for being such a rotten sport?" he said contritely.

She squeezed him to her breast. "No, silly! How can I hate you?" she whispered. "You see, I have a confession to make, too. When—when I suggested gambling for possession of the picture, and—and put myself up as the other half of the bet—I wanted to lose. And so—"

She held out an object for him to see. It was the coin she had tossed. He looked at it. *It was tails on both sides!*

Kitty's Kisses

[*Continued from page* 31]

was—shocked. For never before had Kitty refused him a kiss.

Seeing his pained expression, Kitty relented somewhat.

"You may kiss me on the cheek," she granted.

Reggie did so.

"You may kiss me anywhere," Kitty continued, "except on the lips."

Reggie looked his wonder, but didn't stop to ask why.

"Anywhere?" he repeated in a daze.

"Well . . . almost anywhere," Kitty compromised.

Reggie needed no further invitation. He swept Kitty into his arms with a force she had hitherto thought him incapable of; his lips found her forehead, her cheeks, her chin, her eyes—they were everywhere at once, while endearing words poured from him in the intervals when he was not kissing her madly. But whenever his lips approached hers, she turned her head away.

Now nothing ever seems as important as a kiss that cannot be obtained. So Reggie kept putting his lips near hers, hoping against hope that she would give in to their importunities. But she was adamant.

"Reggie," she cried, "you know how much I care for you! And tonight more than ever before—"

She sank into his embrace, careless of the fact that her flimsy frock, the shoulder straps of which had fallen, began slowly to make its descent down the delightful curves of her fresh young body. Reggie was not slow to aid the laws of gravitation, and soon Kitty was sans her frock, looking lovely as a dream in her panties and brassiere.

In every love affair, there is a moment of full realization. At this moment, though Reggie had often thought, previously, that he loved Kitty, he *knew* that he loved her. And the knowledge brought a new keen thrill to his jaded senses, keyed his emotions to a point unbearable.

So although Kitty was amenable to his embraces, and didn't in the least mind his most ardent caresses, Reggie was not satisfied.

Her body was more beautiful, it seemed to him, than any that could be modeled by a great sculptor; and it was his to feast on with his eyes; but yet—

Reggie knew that all his delight, all his love, was as nothing if not sealed by a kiss. For the kiss is the eternal property of love; embraces, be they ever so ardent, are to the sensitive soul very little when unaccompanied by a meeting of the lips. Kisses are the poetry of love.

"Won't you let me kiss you, darling?" Reggie pleaded. "Somehow I can't—can't look at you in all your beauty—can't touch you—without—"

"Poor boy," sympathized Kitty. "I am sorry I can't—but somehow—"

Again she was close to him, again he felt her heart palpitating against his chest.

And then it happened. Her lips met his.

She sank back against him, resignation in her eyes.

"I have to kiss you," she said, simply, "even if I don't want to."

Reggie's heart bounded.

"I'm so happy!" he said. "But what makes you so averse to kissing me? I can't understand it at all."

Poor Kitty! A lump came into her throat. She didn't want to tell, but what use was there? "It's because," she faltered, trying to make some sort of explanation, "because —I've kissed so many—so many men, and—"

"That's nothing! I've known lots of girls, too. Nowadays—"

"But you don't grasp what I mean! I've—"

Reggie almost fell with surprise when Kitty finished telling him. But a moment later, he looked her in the eyes and said softly: "May I have all your kisses—every one of them left—*for life?*"

"Yes," answered Kitty.

When Reggie had gone, she sat down to write a letter. It was addressed to the Charity Bazaar, and began as follows: "I am sorry, but I must give up that Buy-A-Kiss Counter. After those four hundred and fifty men that bought kisses yesterday, my lips were so tired that—"

It ended, roguishly: "Besides, I can't possibly appear, as I'm under contract anyway."

Read Learning To Love, *by Jack Woodford, in the next SNAPPY; A Zippy, Sophisticated Story Full of Spice and Sparkle.*

The Love Hunt

[*Continued from page* 48]

"This is all, it just can't get any better!" he assured himself as he opened the new envelope.

He was right. For the insert merely said:

GO HOME AND GO TO BED.

Roger obeyed. It was a good idea. He was tired of this treasure hunt anyway. And once safe in bed he could feast his memory on the vision of delight he had saved from the speakeasy raid. That would be a lot better than playing around with girls who did not interest him.

Reaching his pent-house, he was about to ring when he remembered that this was his man's night off. He let himself in and strolled to his bedroom.

Suddenly he stopped dead. There was a light in the room. And—Cautiously peering in, Roger gasped.

For the girl was none other than the burning blue-eyed baby of the night of the raid.

"Who—what?" burbled Roger.

She smiled, a bit timorously. "So you—you escaped after all?" she said.

"Escaped—do I look like a jail-bird?"

"I mean—escaped the perils I put in your path tonight, the girls who tried to have you make love to them," she lisped.

"You mean—that treasure-hunt?" he gasped.

She laughed merrily. "There wasn't any treasure-hunt. It was just a scheme I made up for testing you. When you were looking for me in the bushes that night, I was in back of your car memorizing your license-plates. I looked you up, Mr. Roger Ashley. I—I liked you at first sight, but I wanted to be sure of you. I don't care for men who make love to every girl they meet. So to see if you cared enough for me to forget other girls, I planned this treasure-hunt for one—with Lola's help. Yes, she's an old friend of mine. She knew your man wouldn't be in tonight. I figured that if you really loved me, you wouldn't let Christine, Doris, or Madge delay you—as I asked them to try."

"The soprano, the bartender, the pint-sized brunette!"

"Uh huh. And I reckoned that with you out treasure-hunting, I could safely sneak in here through the window. If one of the girls attracted you, I knew you wouldn't get back here tonight. And if you did get back, it would mean you were a one-man girl after all, and in that case—well, it would be nice."

Roger took one stride towards her. And—

Was it nice? I ask you.

Malou Gets Her Man

[*Continued from page* 29]

"How do you feel this morning?" Howard asked anxiously so soon as they were alone.

"I've got the devil of a headache," she told him. "What happened anyway? Why did you go away and leave me; I might have died."

"You were alive enough when I left you," he told her in surprise. "You don't remember a single thing about my reviving you, and giving you an, er—treatment?"

"What kind of treatment?" she asked, with wide, blue innocent eyes.

"Why, er—first aid," he stammered. "I am astounded that you don't remember."

"Tell me all about it," she begged.

"I will," he promised; "but there's something I wish you'd do first. . . . And that is, jump into the car with me, I want to run you into town."

Presently they were at the rectory of a small church near the city hall. A minister, glad of the chance to be of service, performed the marriage ceremony.

"Now," he told her that night, "I shall inform you as to my method of treating girls who have been bumped upon the head in swimming pools. In order fully to appreciate what happened, you'll have to get into the condition that you were in last night." She did.

"The treatment," he began, "went something like this." He started kissing her violently. But the treatment was no news to Malou; for, of course, she had never actually bumped her head at all in the first place.

Are You Happily Married?

This Scientific Discovery Paves The Way To Health and Happiness

Hygiene Facts FREE

It is no longer necessary for women to suffer from so many physical ailments and handicaps peculiar to their sex. Modern science offers instant relief and protection so that women of today may be free from most feminine ills and discomforts. You can relieve your mind from all worry and unhappiness and enjoy your married life to its fullest extent. On health depends the youthful freshness, vitality and eagerness to do things which characterizes the popular and successful woman. EVERY WOMAN desires to achieve this end and every woman can through the use of the scientific discovery offered here.

Dont Take Unnecessary Chances With Your Health and Happiness!

It is old fashioned to take unnecessary chances with your health and happiness. It is old fashioned to say that ignorance is bliss. There is no need for the modern woman to remain ignorant—there is no need for her to continually risk and gamble with her health and happiness. A thorough understanding of feminine hygiene which can be easily understood and practised through the Dupree method offers you the protection for your health and happiness that you have long sought. Seek no longer, because all of this is now within your reach. Feminine hygiene simply means the keeping of vaginal passages antiseptically clean. This can be accomplished through our simple directions and the use of our famous Dupree Vagi-cones and Dupree Tabs.

Dupree's French Specific Pills of Pennyroyal, Tansy and Cottonroot have been standard for 35 years and recommended by many physicians. Don't take unnecessary chances any longer. Place your order for this treatment today.

Convincing Proof from Users

Below you will find reproduced a few of the many testimonials we received. Because of the personal nature of our treatment, we do not publish the actual names or addresses. The original letters may be seen by any doubting individual at our office.

DOCTOR RECOMMENDS DUPREE

Doctor ——— of Hartford as reference. Please send Dupree pills as soon as possible. Mrs. V., New York.

BEST SHE EVER USED

Please send a box of Dupree pills. My wife says they are the best she ever used. W. M., Pennsylvania.

CLOSE FRIEND TELLS HER

Dupree pills have been highly recommended to me by a very close friend. I would like to have a box very much. A. E. A., Illinois.

CERTAINLY HELPED

Please send me two boxes of Dupree pills. I like to keep them on hand as they certainly helped me. Mrs. A. B., Connecticut.

COMPLETE SATISFACTION

Send me at once your Dupree's French Specific Pills. I have a number of friends to whom I will recommend the remedy as I have used them before with complete satisfaction. Mrs. T. P., Michigan.

WANTS SPECIAL COMBINATION

Enclosed find order for Vagi-cones and Tabs, also box of pills. Tried your pills and think they are fine. Mrs. E. P., New York City.

ORDERS COMBINATION FOR WIFE

Enclosed please find $3.00 for one of your complete treatments. Your treatment has been highly recommended to my wife. Mr. W. M., New York.

Special Combination Offer

Dupree antiseptic Vagi-cones are extensively used as a germ destroyer and are used without the slightest inconvenience. PRICE $1.00 a box (6 boxes $5.00).

Dupree TABS are most effective and safe antiseptic to insure immaculate cleanliness for women—non-poisonous and will not injure or irritate but destroy germs. Price per large box $1.00 (6 boxes $5.00).

DUPREE PILLS are a scientific combination of Pennyroyal, Tansy and Cottonroot and stands out as the most beneficial specific indicated in conditions of female disorders. Their action is mild and causes no ill after-effects. Price $2.00 per box (3 boxes $5.00).

You can order any of the above singularly or the entire combination for $3.00 which means a saving of $1.00 to you on this order. Rush coupon today.

DUPREE MEDICAL CO., Dept. 308
18 WARREN STREET -:- NEW YORK

Dupree Products Are Guaranteed

Testimonials from everywhere prove that Dupree products are all that we claim for them. The fact that many physicians recommend them proves that they are safe and harmless. We in turn guarantee entire satisfaction or money refunded. All we ask is that you give the treatment a trial so that you may know how to live a sane, free and enjoyable life. In order to get acquainted and to introduce our treatment to new friends, we are making a special combination offer which is explained below. Take advantage of the special combination offer, not only because it affords a savings in dollars and cents, but it assures you of the utmost protection, comfort and happiness. Order today—NOW! Before you forget.

Rush Coupon or Ask Your Druggist

DUPREE MEDICAL CO.,
Dept. 308, 18 Warren St., New York

I accept the offer I have checked below, for which I am enclosing remittance of $...........

- ☐ Offer No. 1—combination offer as explained $3.00
- ☐ Offer No. 2—Dupree Vagi-cones $1.00 (6 boxes for $5.00)
- ☐ Offer No. 3—Dupree Tabs $1.00 (6 boxes for $5.00)
- ☐ Offer No. 4—Dupree Pills $2.00 (3 boxes for $5.00)

Kindly send the above postpaid in plain wrapper to address below. Also enclose my free copy of hygiene facts. (If you prefer C. O. D. shipment just sign name and address to coupon, check offer desired and mark X here ☐)

Name..

Street..

City.................................State..............................

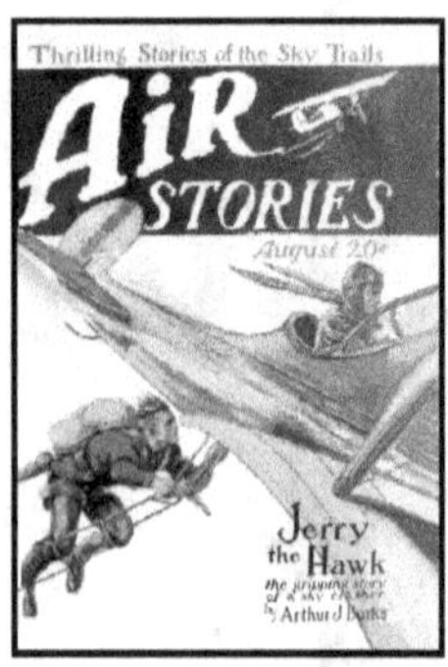
Thrilling Stories of the Sky Trails
Air
STORIES
August 20¢
Jerry the Hawk

AIR
WONDER • STORIES

Fantastic and Weird
CLASSICS #1
WEIRD TALES
"OOZE"

Science Fiction
CLASSICS
AMAZING
STORIES
BLACK PIRATES of BARSOOM
by EDGAR RICE BURROUGHS

COMET

EXCITING
WESTERN
TAKE A REST RANGER
Shadows on THE RAFTER R
By W. C. TUTTLE

THE MAN FROM MARS
fantastic
ADVENTURES
REVOLT of the ROBOTS

FICTION AND FACT OF THE PRIZE-RING
FIGHT
STORIES
September 20c
THE BLACK UHLAN

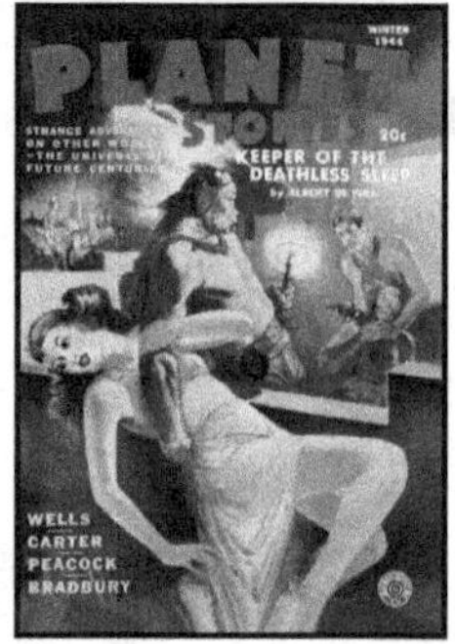
PLANET
STORIES
KEEPER OF THE DEATHLESS SLEEP
WELLS
CARTER
PEACOCK
BRADBURY

The Illustrated
DETECTIVE MAGAZINE
THE WOMAN WHO PAID with her Life
Why Vivian Gordon Was Murdered
The Hollywood BRIDAL-NIGHT MURDER
THE SCARLET FAN

IMAGINATION
SCIENCE and FANTASY
FIRST ISSUE
THE SOUL STEALERS

SEPT.
25¢
SPICY-ADVENTURE
STORIES
DRAGON of KAO TSU

Spicy
STORIES
September
1933
25c

SHANGHAI STAKES, another HILA story
SCARLET
ADVENTURESS
OCT.
25c
SATAN'S

CAPTAIN
FUTURE
WIZARD OF SCIENCE
15¢
CAPT. FUTURE AND THE SPACE EMPEROR

MYSTERY-ADVENTURE-ROMANCE
WONDER
Stories

ARMY
Romances

Science
Fiction
QUARTERLY
SUMMER 1940
SPACE-SHIP DERBY

FIGHTING ACES OF WAR SKIES
WINGS
20c

THRILLING
WONDER
STORIES
15¢
WORLDS WITHIN WORLDS

www.ingramcontent.com/pod-product-compliance
Lightning Source LLC
LaVergne TN
LVHW061254100826
845148LV00008B/1122

* 9 7 8 1 6 4 7 2 0 2 4 3 9 *